WITHDRAWN

NOTEBOOKS
1942 – 1951

———

NOTEBOOKS

1942 – 1951

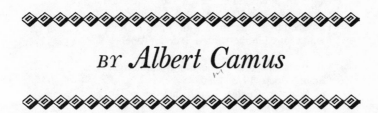

BY *Albert Camus*

TRANSLATED FROM THE FRENCH
AND ANNOTATED BY
JUSTIN O'BRIEN

Marlowe & Company
New York

First Marlowe & Company edition, 1995

Published in the United States by
Marlowe & Company
632 Broadway, Seventh Floor
New York, New York 10012

Originally published in French under the title *Carnets,
janvier 1942–mars 1951*. © 1964, Editions Gallimard.
Published by arrangement with Alfred A. Knopf, Inc.
Manufactured in the United States of America

Library of Congress Cataloging-in-Publication Data
Camus, Albert, 1913–1960.
    [Carnets. English. Selections]
    Notebooks, 1942–1951 / by Albert Camus :
translated from the French and annotated by
Justin O'Brien.
        p.   cm.
    Translation of: Carnets, janvier 1942-mars 1951.
    Reprint. Originally published : New York : Knopf,
c1965.
        ISBN 1-56924-967-9   : $10.95
        1. Camus, Albert, 1913–1960—Notebooks,
sketchbooks, etc.
    I. O'Brien, Justin, 1906–1968.   II. Title.
    PQ2605.A3734Z464   1991b
    848'.91403—dc20   91–3258
                                                 CIP

This book is printed on acid-free paper
Manufactured in the United States of America

EDITORS' NOTE

(from the French edition)

THIS SECOND VOLUME of the *Notebooks* raised some problems. Albert Camus had left a typewritten copy, which he had not corrected. In order to establish the text, Mme Albert Camus and M. Roger Quilliot went back to an earlier typescript, partially corrected by the author, and to the manuscript. This settled most of the problems. In the few cases where an uncertainty remains, a note calls attention to it. The text is given *in toto,* except for eighteen lines (p. 200) concerning the health of a living person. Likewise, a few names had to be replaced by X. Two passages that Albert Camus had transferred to other files for later use have been reintegrated in the text, as the notes indicate.

The accounts of the trips Albert Camus made to North America (March to May 1946) and South America (June to August 1949) constitute a real travel book; therefore it seemed more logical to publish them later in a separate volume.

CONTENTS

NOTEBOOK IV

January 1942 – September 1945

"Whatever does not kill me strengthens me." Yes, but . . . And how painful it is to dream of happiness. The crushing weight of it all. Better to say nothing and pay attention to everything else.

A dilemma, Gide says, between morality and sincerity. And again: "The only beautiful things are those that madness prompts and reason writes."

I must break with everything. If there is no desert at hand there is always the plague or Tolstoy's little railway station.

Goethe: "I felt myself God enough to descend to the daughters of men."

There are no great crimes of which an intelligent man does not feel capable. According to Gide, great minds do not give in to this *because they would limit themselves by so doing.*[1]

Retz[2] readily calms an initial uprising in Paris because it is suppertime. "The most excited don't want to upset their schedule."

Foreign landmarks
{
Tolstoy
Melville
D. Defoe
Cervantes
}

Retz: "With the exception of courage, the Duc d'Or-léans had everything that is essential to a gentleman."
Aristocrats during the Fronde meeting a funeral procession charged the crucifix with drawn swords shouting: "There's the enemy."

There are many reasons behind the official hostility toward England (good or bad, political or not). But nothing

[1] This reference to Gide, like the earlier one and the quotation from Goethe, alludes to *The Journals of André Gide* (Alfred A. Knopf, 1947), Vol. I, pp. 71, 19, 38, and 31, originally published in French in 1939.
[2] Paul de Gondi, Cardinal de Retz (1613–79), played a part in the revolt of the Fronde, which he recorded in his lively *Mémoires*.

is said of one of the worst motives—fury and the base desire to see the downfall of someone who dares to resist the force that has crushed you.

The Frenchman has preserved the habit and traditions of revolution.[3] The only thing he lacks is guts: he has become civil servant, Philistine, *midinette*. It was a stroke of genius to make of him a legal revolutionary. He indulges in plotting with official approval. He reshapes a world without stirring from his easy chair.

Epigraph for "Oran or the Minotaur."[4]
Gide, *An Unprejudiced Mind:* "I fancy him at the court of Minos, anxious to know what sort of unmentionable monster the Minotaur may be, whether he is as frightful as all that or perhaps charming?"

In ancient drama, the one who pays is always the one who is right—Prometheus, Oedipus, Orestes, etc. But that's not important. Anyway they all end in Hades, right or wrong. There is neither reward nor punishment. This explains, to our eyes clouded over by centuries of Christian perversion, the gratuitous nature of those dramas—and also the pathos of such plays.

Contrast Gide's remark: "The great danger is to let one-self be monopolized by a fixed idea" with Nietzschian "obe-

---

3 Instead of *révolution*, the manuscript originally had *grande pensée* ("great thought").
4 The following epigraph, which appears in the original Algiers edition of *L'Été* in 1939, was omitted from the later Paris edition.

dience." Gide again, speaking of the underprivileged: "Leave them eternal life or give them revolution." For my essay on revolt. "Don't take me out of my dear little grotto," the Poitiers girl locked up by her parents said of the room in which she lived surrounded by dung.[5]

The pull that justice and its absurd procedure has for certain minds—Gide, Dostoevsky, Balzac, Kafka, Malraux, Melville, etc. Find the explanation.

Stendhal. One can imagine the story of Malatesta or of the Este family told by Barrès and then by Stendhal. Stendhal would adopt the style of the historical chronicle, the reportage of the "great writer." It is in the disproportion between the tone and the story that Stendhal's secret lies (compare with certain Americans). Just the same disproportion that exists between Stendhal and Beatrice Cenci. Unsuccessful if Stendhal had adopted the tone of pathos (despite literary histories, Tyrtaeus is comic and hateful). *The Red and the Black* has as a subtitle "Chronicle of 1830." *Italian Chronicles*, etc.

MARCH

Milton's Lucifer:

> Farthest from Him is best . . .
> The mind is its own place, and in itself
> Can make a Heav'n of Hell, a Hell of Heav'n.
> . . . .
> Better to reign in Hell, than serve in Heaven.

[5] See *La Séquestrée de Poitiers* (1930) by André Gide.

Brief psychology of Adam and Eve: he formed for contemplation and courage; she for softness and alluring grace. He for God alone; she for God in him.

Schiller dies "having saved all that could be saved."

Book X of the *Iliad*. Those leaders sapped by insomnia, their defeat unbearable, changing their minds, wandering, loving one another, banding together to seek adventure, a raid on the enemy "just for the hell of it."

The horses of Patrocles weep in battle, their master being dead. And (Book XVIII) Achilles' three great shouts on his return to battle, standing over the defense ditch, dazzling in his arms, fierce. And the Trojans retreat. Book XXIV. Achilles' grief as he weeps in the night after the victory. Priam: "For I have done what no man has done on earth—I have lifted to my mouth the hands of the man who killed my children."

(Nectar was red!)

The highest praise that can be given the *Iliad* is that, knowing the outcome of the fight, we nevertheless agonize with the Achaeans behind their lines of defense hard pressed by the Trojans. (Same observation for the *Odyssey;* we know that Ulysses will kill the suitors.) What a thrill for those who heard the tale for the first time!

X For a generous psychology.

We help a person more by giving him a favorable image of himself than by constantly reminding him of his shortcomings. Each individual normally strives to resemble his best image. Can be applied to teaching, to history, to philosophy, to politics. We are for instance the result of twenty centuries of Christian imagery. For two thousand years man has been offered a humiliating image of himself. The result is obvious. Anyway, who can say what we should be if those twenty centuries had clung to the ancient ideal with its beautiful human face?

In the psychoanalyst's view, the ego is constantly putting on a show for itself, but the libretto is false.

F. Alexander and H. Staub. *The Criminal*.[6] Centuries ago, people affected by hysteria were condemned; there will come a time when criminals will be treated.

"Live and die in front of a mirror," Baudelaire says. The words "and die" are not sufficiently noticed. As for living, everyone agrees. But to be master of one's death, that is the hard thing.

Psychosis of arrest.[7] He regularly frequented smart public places—concert halls, famous restaurants. Creating bonds, a solidarity with the people there, is a defense in itself. And it's warm rubbing elbows with others. He dreamed of publishing impressive books that would surround his name with a halo and make him untouchable. All that was needed, he thought, was to get the cops to read his books. They'd say: "But that fellow has great sensitivity. He's an artist. You can't condemn such a soul." But at

---

6 *The Criminal, the Judge, and the Public* by Franz Alexander and Hugo Staub, originally published in Vienna in 1929.

7 See the character of Cottard in *The Plague*, last chapter of I.

other times he felt that an ailment, some infirmity, would protect him just as much. And just as criminals used to flee to deserted places, he made plans to flee to a hospital, a sanatorium, a nursing home.

He needed contact and warmth. He counted up his contacts. "Impossible for them to do that to the friend of Mr. X, the guest of Mr. Y." But there were never enough contacts to stay the calm arm that threatened him. So he would turn to epidemics. Just suppose typhus, a plague— such things happen. It's plausible in a way. Well, all is changed; the desert has come to you. No one has time any more to be concerned with you. Because that's it: the idea that someone, without your knowing it, is concerned with you and you don't know how far he has got, what he has decided, and even if he has decided. Then the plague— and I'm not talking of earthquakes.

Thus that wild heart called on his fellow men and begged their warmth. Thus that furrowed, shriveled soul sought fresh waters in the desert and found peace in an ailment, a curse, and catastrophes. (To be expanded.)

A.B.'s grandfather decided at the age of fifty that he had done enough. In his little house in Tlemcen he took to bed and never got up again, except for essentials, until his death at eighty-four. He was so stingy he had never even bought a watch. He measured time and especially mealtimes by two pots, one of which was filled with chickpeas.[8] He would fill the other using a careful, mechanical motion and thus have his guide marks in a day measured in pots.

He had already given signs of his vocation by the fact that nothing interested him, not his work, nor friendship, nor music, nor the café. He had never left his home town except once when, obliged to go to Oran, he got off at the

[8] See the old asthmatic in *The Plague,* sixth chapter of II.

station nearest to Tlemcen, frightened by the adventure. He then returned home by the first train. To those who were astonished by his life during the thirty-four years he spent in bed, he used to say that religion stipulated that half a man's life was an ascent and the other half a descent and that in the descent his days were no longer his. Moreover, he contradicted himself by pointing out that God did not exist, for if he did the existence of priests would have been useless, but such a philosophy was attributed to the anger he felt at the frequent passing of the plate in his parish.

To cap it all was his profound wish, which he repeated to everyone, to live to a very old age.

Is there a tragic dilettantism?

Once he has reached the absurd and tries to live *accordingly,* a man always perceives that consciousness is the hardest thing in the world to maintain. Circumstances are almost always against it. He must live his lucidity in a world where dispersion is the rule.

So he perceives that the real problem, *even without God,* is the problem of psychological unity (the only problem really raised by the operation of the absurd is that of the metaphysical unity of the world and the mind) and inner peace. He also perceives that such peace is not possible without a discipline difficult to reconcile with the world. *That's where the problem lies.* It must indeed be reconciled with the world. It is a matter of achieving *a rule of conduct in secular life.*

The great obstacle is *his past life* (profession—marriage—previous opinions, etc.). What has already taken place.

Not to elude any of the elements of this problem.

Hateful, the writer who talks about and exploits what he has never experienced. But be careful, a murderer is not the best man to talk of crime. (But isn't he the best man to talk of *his* crime? Even that is not certain.) Essential to imagine a certain distance between creation and the deed. The true artist stands midway between what he imagines and what he does. He is the one who is "capable of." He could be what he describes, experience what he writes. The mere act would limit him; he would be the one who has acted.

"Superiors never forgive their inferiors for possessing the external signs of greatness." *The Country Curate.*

Id. "There's no more bread." Véronique and the Valley of Montignac grow at *the same rate.* Same symbolism as in *The Lily in the Valley.*

For those who say that Balzac writes badly, see the death of Mme Graslin: "Everything in her was purified and illuminated, and on her face shone a reflection of the flaming swords held by the guardian angels surrounding her."

Study of a Woman: The tale is impersonal, but Bianchon is relating it.

Alain[9] on Balzac: "His genius consists in taking the commonplace as his subject and making it sublime without changing it."

Balzac and cemeteries in *Ferragus.*

Balzac's baroque quality: the pages on the organ in Ferragus and the *Duchess of Langeais.*

[9] Alain (pseud. of Émile Chartier, 1868–1951) exerted a great influence through his teaching and his philosophical and literary essays.

That flame of which the Duchess sees the glowing and dim reflection at Montriveau's glows throughout the work of Balzac.

There are two kinds of style: Mme de La Fayette's and Balzac's. The first is perfect in detail; the second works in the mass and even four chapters barely give an idea of its force. Balzac writes well not *despite* but *because of* his errors in grammar.

Secret of my universe: imagining God without human immortality.

Charles Morgan and singleness of mind:[1] the felicity of the single intention—the sure talent of excellence—"genius is this power of dying"—opposition to woman and her tragic love of life—so many themes, so many nostalgias.

Shakespeare's sonnets:
"Looking on darkness which the blind do see."
"To this I witness call the fools of time,
Which die for goodness, who have lived for crime."

The lands that shelter beauty are the hardest to defend —so eager are people to spare them. Thus artistic nations ought to be the natural victims of barren nations—if the love of freedom did not outweigh the love of beauty in men's hearts. That is an instinctive wisdom, freedom being the source of beauty.

[1] The English writer Charles Morgan (1894–1958) prefaced his play *The Flashing Stream* in 1938 with a long essay "On Singleness of Mind."

Calypso offers Ulysses a choice between immortality and the land of his birth. He rejects immortality. Therein lies perhaps the whole meaning of the *Odyssey*. In Book XI, Ulysses and the dead facing the ditch full of blood, and Agamemnon says to him: "Be not too good to your wife and do not confide all your thoughts to her."

Note also that the *Odyssey* speaks of Zeus as the Creator. A dove falls on the rock "but the Father creates another one so that the number will be full."

XVII—The dog Argos.

XXII—The women who have given themselves are hanged—unbelievable cruelty.

Again for Stendhal as a chronicler—See *Journal*, pp. 28–9.

"The height of passion may be to kill a fly for one's mistress." "Only women with strong character can make me happy."

And this touch: "As often happens with men who have concentrated their energy on one or two vital points, he had an indolent and casual manner."

Vol. II: "I felt so intensely this evening that I have a stomach ache."

Stendhal, who was not wrong about his own literary future, was lamentably wrong about Chateaubriand's: "I shall bet that in 1913 his writings will be forgotten."

Heinrich Heine's epitaph: "He loved the roses of the Brenta."

Flaubert: "A man judging another is a sight that would make me burst with laughter if it did not fill me with pity."

What he saw at Genoa: "a marble city with rose-filled gardens."

And: "Folly consists in trying to draw conclusions."

Flaubert's *Correspondence:*

Vol. II: "Success with women is generally a sign of mediocrity." (?)

X *Id.* "Live as a common man and think as a demi-god." (??) See the story of the tapeworm.

"Masterpieces are stupid; they have the calm exterior of big animals."

"If I had been loved at seventeen, what an artist I should be now!"

"In art, one must never fear being *exaggerated* . . . But the exaggeration must be continuous—in proportion to itself."[2]

His aim: ironic acceptance of existence and its total recasting through art. "Living doesn't concern us."

Explain the man by this far-reaching, key remark: "I maintain that cynicism leads to chastity."

Id. "We should accomplish nothing in this world if we were not guided by wrong ideas." (Fontenelle)

At first sight a man's life is more interesting than his works. It constitutes an obstinate, taut whole. Unity of

2 At the top of the manuscript page is written: "See Berlioz correspondence. Theologico-political treatise."

mind dominates. There is a single inspiration through all those years. He *is* the novel. To be rewritten, obviously.

There is always a philosophy for lack of courage.

Art criticism, through fear of being classed as literature, tries to speak the language of painting, and then it becomes literary. One has to go back to Baudelaire. Human transposition, *but objective.*

Mme V. surrounded by smells of rotting meat. Three cats, two dogs. Discoursing about inner melody. The kitchen is closed; it is frightfully hot there.

The whole sky and the heat weigh heavily upon the bay. All is luminous. But the sun has disappeared.

The difficulties of solitude are to be treated fully.

Montaigne: a life that slips past, somber and mute life.

Modern intelligence is in utter confusion. Knowledge has become so diffuse that the world and the mind have lost all point of reference. It is a fact that we are suffering from nihilism. But the most amazing things are the admonitions to "turn backward."[3] Return to the Middle Ages, to primitive mentality, to the soil, to religion, to the arsenal of worn-out solutions. To grant a shadow of efficacy to

[3] Allusion to the speeches and writings of the Vichy period.

those panaceas, we should have to act as if our acquired knowledge had ceased to exist, as if we had learned nothing, and pretend in short to erase what is inerasable. We should have to cancel the contribution of several centuries and the incontrovertible acquisitions of a mind that has finally (in its last step forward) re-created chaos on its own. That is impossible. In order to be cured, we must make our peace with this lucidity, this clairvoyance. We must take into account the glimpses we have suddenly had of our exile. Intelligence is in confusion not because knowledge has changed everything. It is so because it cannot accept that change. It hasn't "got accustomed to that idea." When this does happen, the confusion will disappear. Nothing will remain but the change and the clear knowledge that the mind has of it. There's a whole civilization to be reconstructed.

Any proofs must be palpable.

"Europe," Montesquieu said, "will be lost by its military men."

Who can say: I have had a perfect week? My memory tells me so and I know it doesn't lie. Yes, the image is perfect as those long days were perfect. Purely physical joys with the mind's consent. There lies perfection, harmony with one's condition, man's gratitude and respect.

Wild and pure sloping dunes! Glory of the water, so black in the morning, so clear at noon, and warm and gilded in the evening. Long mornings on the dune among naked bodies, and immediately everything has to be repeated, everything said that has been said. There was youth. There is youth and, at the age of thirty, I want nothing else but such youth to continue. But . . .

The writings of Copernicus and Galileo remained on the Index until 1822. Three centuries of obstinacy; it really is touching.

Capital punishment. The criminal is killed because the crime has spent all the capacity for living a man has. He has experienced everything if he has killed. He can die. Murder drains a man.

How is the literature of the nineteenth and especially of the twentieth century different from that of classical periods? It too is a moral study because it is French. But classical morality is a critical morality (except for Corneille), hence negative. The morality of the twentieth century on the other hand is positive: it defines *styles of life*. Take the romantic hero, Stendhal (he belongs to his time precisely in this regard), Barrès, Montherlant, Malraux, Gide, etc.

Montesquieu: "Certain kinds of foolishness are such that a greater foolishness would be better."

The "Eternal Return" is easier to understand if it is imagined as a repetition of great moments—as if everything tended to reproduce or echo the climactic moments of humanity. The Italian primitives or the Passion according to St. John reliving, imitating, commenting endlessly on the "It is finished" of Golgotha. Every defeat has in it something of Athens thrown open to the Roman barbarians; every victory reminds us of Salamis, etc., etc.

Brulard: "My writings have always inspired in me the same reticence as my loves."

Id. "A salon of eight or ten persons, where all the women have had lovers, where the conversation is lively and anecdotal and a light punch is served shortly after midnight, is the one place in the world where I am most comfortable."

Psychosis of arrest. On the point of sending his son his allowance, he increased it by a hundred francs. He felt pushed to affection, to generosity. Anxiety makes him altruistic.[4]

Thus the two men hunted down in a city all day long become sentimental as soon as they can talk. One of them weeps, speaking of his wife he has not seen in two years. Imagine evenings in cities where the hunted man wanders alone.

To J.T. on *The Stranger.*

It's a very studied book and the tone . . . is intentional. The tone is heightened four or five times, to be sure, but this is to avoid monotony and to provide composition. With the Chaplain, my Stranger does not justify himself. He gets angry, and that's quite different. I'm the one to explain

4 See Cottard in *The Plague,* last chapter of I.

then, you say? Yes, and I thought about that considerably. I made up my mind to this because I wanted my character to be led to the single great problem by way of the daily and the natural. The great moment had to stand out. But just notice that there is no break in my character. In that chapter, as in the rest of the book, he limits himself to *answering questions*. Before there were the questions that the world asks us every day; at this moment there are the questions of the Chaplain. So I define my character negatively.

In all this of course I am talking of artistic means and not of the end. The meaning of the book lies precisely in the parallelism of the two parts. Conclusion: society needs people who weep at their mother's funeral; or else one is never condemned for the crime one thinks. Moreover, I see ten other possible conclusions.

Napoleon's great remarks: "Happiness is the greatest development of my faculties."

Before Elba: "A live scoundrel is better than a dead emperor."

"A really great man will always place himself above the events he has caused."

"One must will to live and know how to die."

Criticisms of *The Stranger*. An epidemic of "Moralitis." You fools who think that negation is a forsaking when it is a choice. (The author of *The Plague* shows the heroic side of negation.) There is no other possible life for a man deprived of God; and all men are. Fancying that virility lies in prophetic fidgeting, that greatness lies in spiritual affectation! But that struggle through poetry and its obscurities, that apparent revolt of the mind is *the one that costs least*. It is invalid and tyrants are well aware of this.

Without Sequel[5]

"What am I thinking that is greater than I and that I experience without being able to define it? A sort of arduous progress toward a sanctity of negation—a heroism without God—man alone, in short. All human virtues, including solitude in regard to God.

"What constitutes the *exemplary* superiority (the only one) of Christianity? Christ and his saints; pursuit of a *style of life*. My work will count as many forms as it has stages on the way to an unrewarded perfection. *The Stranger* is the zero point. Likewise *The Myth of Sisyphus*. *The Plague* is a progress, not from zero toward the infinite, but toward a deeper complexity that remains to be defined. The last point will be the saint, but he will have his arithmetical value, measurable like man."

Concerning criticism. Three years to make a book, five lines to ridicule it, and the quotations wrong.

Letter to A.R., literary critic (fated not to be sent) . . . One sentence in your criticism struck me: "I am not taking into account . . ." How can an enlightened critic, aware of the careful planning that goes into any work of art, fail to take into account, in the depiction of a character, the *sole moment* when he talks about himself and entrusts the reader with some of his secret? And how could you fail to feel that that ending was also a convergence, a privileged

---

[5] It appears that *sans lendemain* (which might be rendered "without sequel") was added to the manuscript after a rereading.

spot for the fragmented creature I have described to come together at last . . .

. . . You attribute to me an ambition to be realistic. Realism is an empty word (*Madame Bovary* and *The Possessed* are both realistic novels and they have nothing in common). I never thought of such a thing. If a label had to be given to my ambition, I should speak rather of the symbol. You were well aware of this, moreover. But you attribute to that symbol a meaning it does not have and, in short, you have gratuitously attributed to me a ridiculous philosophy. Nothing in the book, in fact, can allow you to assert that I believe in the natural man, that I identify a human being with a vegetable, that human nature is foreign to morality, etc., etc. The chief character in the book never takes an initiative. You didn't notice that he always limits himself to *answering questions*, those asked by life or those asked by men. Hence he never asserts anything. And I gave only a negative snapshot of him. Nothing could make you leap to a presumption as to his deeper attitude except, it so happens, the last chapter. But you "are not taking it into account."

The reasons for my insistence on "saying the minimum" would be too long to give you. But I can at least regret that a superficial reading prompted you to attribute to me a philosophy of the man in the street that I am not ready to assume. You will be more aware of what I am stating if I point out that the only quotation in your article is wrong (give it and correct it) and that it consequently serves as a basis for illegitimate deductions. Perhaps there was another philosophy and you were close to it when describing the word "inhumanity." But what is the use of pointing this out?

You will think perhaps that I'm making much ado over a short book by an unknown writer. But I believe that this affair goes beyond me. For you have taken a moral point of view that prevented you from judging with the lucidity and the talent you have been known for. Your position is untenable and you know it better than anyone. There is a very vague frontier between your criticisms and the judgments that may soon be made by a dictatorship (that were made in France not so long ago) as to the moral character of this or that work. Let me tell you without anger, that is hateful. Neither you nor anyone has a right to judge whether a work may serve or harm the nation at this moment or forever. I refuse in any case to submit to such judgments, and this is the reason for my letter. I beg you to believe, indeed, that I should have accepted more serious criticisms with serenity if they had been expressed in a less didactic spirit.

In any case I hope that this letter will not lead to a new misunderstanding. I am not indulging here in the protest of a discontented writer. I beg you not to allow any of this letter to be published. You have not seen my name often in the periodicals, though they are not difficult of access. This is because, having nothing to say in them, I do not like sacrificing to publicity. I am publishing at present books that took years of work, simply because they are now finished, and I am planning the next manuscript. I am not expecting any material advantage or any consideration from them. I merely hoped that they would win me the attention and patience granted to anything undertaken in good faith. Apparently even that hope was excessive. Nevertheless, please believe me, sir . . . Yours sincerely.

Three characters entered into the composition of *The Stranger:* two men (I am one) and one woman.

Brice Parain. Essay on the Platonic logos.[6] Studies the logos as speech. Ends up by endowing Plato with a philosophy of expression. Traces Plato's effort in pursuit of a reasonable realism. What is the "tragic" element of the problem? If our speech has no meaning, nothing has meaning. If the sophists are right, the world is mad. Plato's solution is not psychological; it is cosmological. What is the originality of Parain's position? He considers the problem of speech as metaphysical rather than social and psychological . . . etc., etc. See notes.

French workmen—the only ones among whom I feel at home, whom I want to know and to "live" among. They are like me.

LATE AUGUST '42

Literature. Be wary of that word. Don't pronounce it too fast. If one took literature from great writers, one would remove what is probably most personal to them. Literature = nostalgia. Nietzsche's superman, Dostoevsky's abyss, Gide's gratuitous act, etc., etc.

This sound of babbling springs throughout my days. They flow around me, through sunny fields, then closer to me and soon I shall have this sound in me, that spring in my heart and that sound of a fountain mingled with my every thought. It's forgetfulness.

<hr />

6 A long essay by Camus, "Sur une philosophie de l'expression," in *Poésie 44*, No. 17 (December 1943–February 1944), examines with evident favor the metaphysics of speech elaborated by Brice Parain in *Essai sur le logos platonicien* (1942) and *Recherches sur la nature et les fonctions du langage* (1942).

Plague. Impossible to get away from it. Too many elements of "chance" this time in the composition. I must cling closely to the idea. *The Stranger* describes the nakedness of man facing the absurd. *The Plague,* the basic equivalence of individual points of view facing the same absurd. It's a progress that will become clearer in other works. But in addition *The Plague* shows that the absurd *teaches nothing.* It's a definitive progress.

Panelier.[7] Before sunrise, above the high hills, the fir trees are not distinguishable from the rolling ground on which they stand. Then the sun from a great distance behind them gilds the crest of the trees. Hence against the but slightly faded background of the sky they look like an army of feathered savages rising over the hill. Gradually, as the sun rises and the sky brightens, the fir trees grow larger and the barbarian army seems to move forward and become more compact in a tumult of feathers before the invasion. Then, when the sun is high enough, it suddenly lights up the fir trees, which pour down the slope of the mountains. And it seems like a wild race toward the valley, the outbreak of a brief and tragic battle in which the barbarians of daylight will drive out the fragile army of nocturnal thoughts.

What is touching in Joyce is not the work but the fact of having undertaken it. Need for distinguishing thus the emotional aspect of the undertaking (which has nothing to do with art) and the artistic emotion proper.

[7] For reasons of health, Camus spent several months in the winter and spring of 1942–43 at Panelier, near Le Chambon-sur-Lignon (Haute-Loire), where the altitude is close to 3,000 feet.

Convince oneself that a work of art is a human thing and that the creator has nothing to expect from a transcendental "dictation." *The Charterhouse, Phèdre, Adolphe* might have been quite different—and no less beautiful. All depended on their author, the absolute master.

An essay on France years from now could not do without a reference to the present period. This idea came to me in a little local train[8] as I saw pass by, grouped in front of tiny stations, those French faces and silhouettes I shall never forget: old peasant couples—she with a weathered face and he with a smooth face lighted by two bright eyes and a white mustache, silhouettes that two winters of privations have twisted, dressed in shiny, darned clothing. Elegance has left these people, now inhabited by poverty. On trains their suitcases are worn-out, tied up with strings, patched with cardboard. All the French look like immigrants.

Id. in manufacturing towns. The old workman seated at his window, wearing eyeglasses, taking advantage of the fading daylight to read, his book lying like a good little schoolboy's between his hands flat on the table.

At the station, a mass of hurried people absorb with good grace a vile fare, then go out into the dark town, rub elbows without mingling and go back to their hotels, their rooms, etc. Desolating and silent life that all France endures while waiting.

Around the tenth, the eleventh, the twelfth of the month, everyone smokes. By the eighteenth, impossible to get a light in the streets. In trains everyone is talking of the drought. It is less spectacular than in Algeria but it is no

[8] Every week Camus traveled from Le Chambon-sur-Lignon to Saint-Étienne for medical treatment.

less tragic. An old workman tells of his poverty: his two rooms an hour away from Saint-Étienne. Two hours of travel, eight hours work; nothing to eat at home; too poor to use the black market. A young woman does hours of washing because she has two children and her husband came home from war with a stomach ulcer. "He should have white meat well cooked. Where are you going to get that? He was given a diet certificate. So they give him ¾ of a quart of milk but they won't allow him any fatty matter. Did you ever hear of keeping a man alive on milk?" It sometimes happens that her clients' laundry is stolen, and then she has to pay.

Meanwhile the rain is inundating the squalid landscape of an industrial valley—the pungent smell of that poverty—the dreadful straits of those lives. And the others indulge in speeches.

Saint-Étienne in the morning fog with the factory whistles calling to work amid a jumble of towers, buildings, and tall chimneys belching toward a darkened sky their deposit of cinders—the whole looking like a monstrous artificial cake.

Budejovice, Act III.[9] The sister returns after the mother's suicide. Scene with the wife:

"What gives you a right to speak?"

"My love."

"What's that?"

The sister leaves for her death. The wife screams and weeps. The mute maidservant comes in, drawn by the weeping:

[9] Notes for the next-to-last scene of *The Misunderstanding*, originally entitled *Budejovice*.

"Ah you, you at least will help me!"
"No." (Curtain)

All great virtues have an absurd aspect.

Nostalgia for the life of others. This is because, seen from the outside, another's life forms a unit. Whereas ours, seen from the inside, seems broken up. We are still chasing after an illusion of unity.

Science explains what happens and not what *is*. Ex.: why various species of flowers rather than a single one?

Novel. "He used to wait for her mornings under big hazel bushes in the cold wind of autumn. Buzzing of wasps without summer's heat, the wind in the leaves, a rooster insisting on crowing behind the hills, hollow barkings, at intervals the croaking of a raven. Between the dark September sky and the damp earth, he felt as if he were waiting for winter as well as for Marthe."

Sexual relations with animals suppress the conscience of *the other*. They are "freedom." This is why they have attracted so many minds, even Balzac.

Panelier. First September rain with a slight wind mingling the yellow leaves in the shower. They glide for a moment and then the weight of water they are carrying suddenly flattens them on the ground. When nature is banal as it is here, one is more aware of the change in seasons.

Poor childhood. The raincoat too big—the siesta. The duckling Vinga—Sundays at the aunt's. Books—the public library. Coming home Christmas night and the corpse in front of the restaurant. Games in the cellar (Jeanne, Joseph, and Max). Jeanne picks up every button; "that's the way to become rich." The brother's violin and the singing sessions—Galoufa.

Novel. Don't put "the plague" in the title. But something like "The Prisoners."

Avvakum[1] with his wife on foot in icy Siberia. The Archpriestess: "Shall we have to suffer much longer, Archpriest?" Avvakum: "Daughter of Mark, unto death." And she, sighing: "Very well, son of Peter, then let us keep on walking."

I Corinthians 7:27: "Art thou bound unto a wife? Seek not to be loosed. Art thou loosed from a wife? Seek not a wife."
Luke 6:26: "Woe unto you, when all men shall speak well of you!"

[1] The memoirs of the Archpriest Petrovich Avvakum (1620–82) are considered the earliest Russian autobiography. Twice banished to Siberia as the leader of the Old Believers, Avvakum was finally burned at the stake. His memoirs were published in French in 1938 in a translation by Pierre Pascal.

As an Apostle, Judas performed miracles (St. John Chrysostom).

Chuang Tzu (third of the great Taoists—second half of the fourth century B.C.) has the point of view of Lucretius: "The great bird rises on the wind to a height of 90,000 stadia. What does he see from up there?—herds of wild horses galloping."

Until the Christian era, Buddha is never represented because he is in a state of Nirvana; in other words, depersonalized.

According to Proust, it is not a question of nature imitating art. The great artist teaches us to see in nature what his work, in an individual way, has managed to isolate. All women become Renoirs.[2]

"At the foot of the bed, shaken by all the waves of that death agony, not weeping yet at times bathed in tears, my mother had the inanimate, desolate look of foliage whipped by the rain and twisted by the wind." (*Guermantes*)

"Rarely do the individuals who have played an important part in our life disappear from it suddenly and definitively." (*Guermantes*)

[2] Proust states that after refusing to recognize even the presence of women in Renoir's paintings we come, through familiarity with the new style, to see all women as if they had been painted by Renoir. This and the two following quotations, also from *The Guermantes Way*, may be found in the Pléiade edition in II, pp. 327, 344, and 348 respectively. The quotation that Camus has identified as from *Cities of the Plain* is in II, p. 608.

Remembrance of Things Past is a heroic and virile book

1) by the perseverence of the creative will;
2) by the effort demanded of an invalid.

"When my attacks had forced me to spend several days and nights in succession, not only without sleep, but without lying down, without drinking and without eating, at the moment when exhaustion and pain became such that I thought I should never recover, I would think of a traveler thrown up on the shore, poisoned by deadly weeds, shivering with fever in his clothes soaked by the sea, and who nevertheless felt better after two days, resuming his way at random, in search of any inhabitants whatever, who might be cannibals. His example strengthened me, gave me hope, and I was ashamed of having had a moment of discouragement." (*Cities of the Plain*)

He doesn't go with a prostitute who accosts him and appeals to him because he has nothing but a thousand-franc note on him and doesn't dare ask her for change.

Feeling that is the reverse of Proust's: in reference to every town, every new apartment, every person, every rose and every flame, force oneself to wonder at their novelty while thinking of what habit will do to them; seek in the future the "familiarity" they will give you; go in pursuit of time that has not yet come.

Example: Solitary arrivals at night in strange cities— that sensation of stifling, being transcended by an organism a thousand times more complex. It is enough to locate the main street on the morrow, everything falls into place in relation to it, and we settle in. Collect memories of night arrivals in strange cities, live on the power of those unknown hotel rooms.

In the streetcar: "He was born normal. But a week later his eyelids stuck together. So, of course, his eyes rotted away."

As when we are attracted toward certain cities (almost always those one has already lived in) or certain lives, the images of sex—and then we are taken in. For even the least spiritual among us never live according to sex, or at least there are too many things in everyday life that have nothing to do with sex. So that after having painfully incarnated, and at rare intervals, one of those images or come closer to one of those memories, life is filled with long spaces of empty time like dead skins. And then it is time to long for other cities.

Criticisms on *The Stranger:* Impassivity, they say. The word is bad. Good will would be better.

Budejovice (or God does not answer).[3] The mute maid-servant is an old manservant.

The wife in the last scene: "O Lord, have pity on me. Turn your eyes on me. Hear me, O Lord. Hold out your hand. O Lord, have pity on those who love each other and are separated."

The old man comes in.

"Did you call me?"

[3] Notes for the final scene of *The Misunderstanding.*

The wife: "Yes . . . No . . . I don't know. But help me, help me, for I need to be helped. Have pity and deign to help me."

The old man: "No."

(Curtain)

Look for details to strengthen the symbolism.

How can it be that, linked to such suffering, her face is still the face of happiness for me?

Novel. Beside the dying body of the woman he loves: "I can't, I can't let you die. For I know that I shall forget you. Hence I'll lose everything and I want to keep you on this side of the world, the only one where I am capable of embracing you, etc., etc."

She: "Oh, its a dreadful thing to die knowing one will be forgotten."

Always see and express *at the same time* the two aspects.

Sum up clearly my intentions with *The Plague*.

October. In the still green grass the already yellow leaves. A spasmodic wind was forging with a sonorous sun on the green anvil of the fields a rod of light from which the buzzing of bees reached me. Red beauty.

Splendid, poisonous, and solitary like the red agaric.

There can be seen in Spinoza the love of what is and not of what tends to or is to be—the hatred of values in black and white, of moral hierarchy—a certain equivalence of virtues and evils in the divine light. "Men prefer order to chaos as if order corresponded to something real in nature." (Appendix to Book One)

The inconceivable thing for him would be, not that God created imperfection at the same time as perfection, but that he hadn't created it. For, possessing power to create the whole gamut from the perfect to the imperfect, he could not fail to do so. It's unfortunate only from our point of view, which is not the proper one.

His God, his universe are motionless and their reasons harmonize. Everything is given once and for all. It is up to us, if we so wish, to distinguish the consequences and the reasons (whence the geometric form). But that universe tends toward nothing and comes from nothing because it is already complete and has always been so. It has no tragedy because it has no history. It is consummately inhuman. It is a world for courage.

[A world without art also—because devoid of chance (the Appendix to Book One denies that there is ugliness or beauty).]

Nietzsche says that the mathematical form in Spinoza is justified only as a means of aesthetic expression.

See *Ethics*, Book One. Theorem XI gives four demonstrations of the existence of God. Theorem XIV and the big Scholia of XV which seems to negate creation.

Could justify those who speak of Spinoza's pantheism? Yet it contains a postulate (a word that Spinoza avoids throughout the *Ethics*): the void does not exist (proven, to be sure, in the preceding works).

It is possible to contrast XVII and XXIV: the first proving necessity and the second capable of serving to reintroduce contingency. Theorem XXV establishes the relation between distance and modes. In XXXI, finally, will is limited.

God also by his own nature. XXXIII narrows even more this so restricted world. It would seem that for Spinoza the nature of God is even greater than he; but in Theorem XXXIII he declares (in opposition to the partisans of Sovereign Good) that it is absurd to subject God to fate.

This world is established once and for all; this "is the way it is"—necessity is infinite—originality and chance have no role at all. Everything in it is monotonous.

Strange. Intelligent historians recounting the history of a country bend every effort to praise a certain policy (realistic for instance) to which they attribute that country's great periods. Yet they themselves point out that such a state of affairs has never managed to last because rather soon another statesman or a new regime came along to spoil everything. Nonetheless they persevere in defending a policy that does not resist a change in personalities, whereas politics is made up of a change in personalities. This is because they think and write only for their own era. The alternative to the historians: skepticism or the political theory that does not depend on a change in personalities. (?)

This fine effort is to genius as the jerky flight of the locust is to the flight of the swallow.

"At times, after all those days when will alone directed me, when hour by hour that labor was accomplished which admitted neither distraction nor weakness, which tried to pay no attention to sentiment or the world, ah! what abandon seized me, with what relief I hurled myself into the distress which, all those days, had accompanied me. What a longing, what a temptation to cease being anything that had to be consciously constructed and to forsake the work and the difficult face I had to model. I loved, I had regrets, I desired, I was a man at last . . .

". . . The deserted summer sky, the sea I loved so much, and those lips offered."

Sexual life was given to man to distract him perhaps from his true path. It's his opium. With it everything falls asleep. Outside it, things resume life. At the same time chastity kills the species, which is perhaps the truth.

A writer must never speak of his doubts regarding his creation. It would be too easy to answer him: "Who is forcing you to create? If it is such constant anguish, why do you endure it?" Doubts are the most intimate thing about us. Never speak of one's doubts, *whatever they may be*.

Wuthering Heights, one of the greatest love novels because it ends in failure and revolt—I mean in death without hope. The main character is the devil. Such a love can be maintained only through the ultimate failure that is death. It can continue only in hell.

OCTOBER

The great red forests in the rain, the meadows all covered with yellow leaves, the smell of drying mushrooms, the wood fires (the pine cones reduced to embers glow like infernal diamonds), the wind moaning about the house—

35

where could there be a more conventional autumn? Peasants now walk bent forward, against the wind and the rain.

In the autumn woods, the beeches form spots of golden yellow or stand out on the edge of the woods like big nests flowing with golden honey.

OCTOBER 23. BEGINNING

The Plague has a social meaning *and* a metaphysical meaning. It's exactly the same. Such ambiguity is in *The Stranger* too.

People say: it means no more to him than the life of a fly; and that doesn't speak to the imagination. But if we watch flies dying stuck to flypaper, we realize that the inventor of the device watched at length that dreadful and insignificant death agony, that slow death which barely gives off a slight smell of putrefaction. (Genius is responsible for the commonplace.)

Idea: He rejects everything offered him, every happiness proposed because of a deeper exigence. He ruins his marriage, gets involved in only half-satisfactory liaisons, waits and hopes. "I couldn't really define it, but I feel it." Thus it is to the end of his life. "No, I'll never be able to define it."

Sex leads to nothing. It is not immoral but it is unproductive. One can indulge in it so long as one does not want to produce. But only chastity is linked to a personal progress.

There is a time when sex is a victory—when it is separated from moral imperatives. But soon after it becomes a defeat—and the only victory is then won over it: chastity.

Think of the commentary to Molière's *Don Juan*.[4]

NOVEMBER '42

In the autumn this landscape blossoms with leaves, the cherry trees becoming quite red, the maples yellow, the beeches all bronze. The plateau is covered with the thousand flames of a second spring.

Renouncing youth. I am not the one giving up persons and things (I could not), but rather things and persons are giving me up. My youth is fleeing me; that's what it is to be ill.

The first thing for a writer to learn is the art of transposing what he feels into what he wants to make others feel. The first few times he succeeds by chance. But then talent must take the place of chance. Hence there is an element of chance at the root of genius.

He always says: "It's what in my region would be called . . ." and he adds a trite expression that belongs to no region. Example: It's what in my region would be called ideal weather (or a dazzling career, or a model girl, or poetic lighting).[5]

4 Nothing corresponding to an outline of such a commentary has been found in Camus's files.

5 See Grand's verbal mania in *The Plague*, sixth chapter of I.

NOVEMBER 11. Caught like rats![6]

In the morning everything is covered with hoarfrost; the sky is shining behind the garlands and streamers of an immaculate village fair. At ten o'clock, when the sun begins to warm everything, the whole countryside is filled with the crystalline music of an aerial thaw: little cracklings as if the trees were sighing, fall of the frost on the ground like a sound of white insects dropped on one another, late leaves constantly falling under the weight of the ice and barely bouncing on the ground like weightless bones. All around, the hills and valleys vanish in wisps of smoke. After looking at it for a time, one becomes aware that this landscape, as it loses its colors, had suddenly aged. It is a very ancient landscape returning to us in a single morning through millennia . . . This spur covered with trees and ferns juts out like the prow of a ship into the joining of the two streams. Freed from the hoarfrost by the first rays of the sun, it is the only living thing in this landscape white like eternity. In this spot at least the mingled voices of the two rushing streams join together against the endless silence surrounding them. But gradually the song of the waters is itself fused into the landscape. Without diminishing a jot, it nevertheless becomes silence. And from time to time nothing but the flight of three smoke-colored ravens brings signs of life back into the sky.

Seated at the peak of the prow, I follow that motionless navigation in the land of indifference. Nothing less than all nature and this white peace that winter brings to over-heated hearts—to calm this heart consumed by a bitter love. I watch as this swelling of light spreads over the sky negating the omens of death. Sign of the future in short,

[6] The allied landing in North Africa isolated Camus from family and home.

above me to whom everything now speaks of the past. Keep quiet, lung! Fill yourself with this icy, pure air that feeds you. Keep silent. May I cease being forced to listen to your slow rotting away—and may I turn at last toward . . .

Saint-Étienne

I know what Sunday is for a poor working man. I know especially what a Sunday evening is, and if I could give a meaning and a shape to what I know, I could make of a poor Sunday a work of humanity.

I ought not to have written: if the world were clear, art would not exist—but if the world seemed to me to have a meaning I should not write at all. There are cases when one must be personal, out of modesty. In addition, the remark would have forced me to think it over and, in the end, I should not have written it. It is a brilliant truth, without basis.

Unbridled sex leads to a philosophy of the non-significance of the world. Chastity on the other hand gives the world a meaning.

Kierkegaard. Aesthetic value of marriage. Definitive views but too much verbiage.

Role of ethics and aesthetics in the formation of the personality: much more solid and stirring. Apology for the *general.*

For Kierkegaard aesthetic morality has as an aim originality—and in fact what counts is to achieve the general.

39

Kierkegaard is not mystical. He criticizes mysticism because it stands apart from the world—because it does not belong to the general. If there is a leap in Kierkegaard, it is therefore an intellectual leap. It is the pure leap; on the ethical plane. But the religious plane transfigures everything.

At what moment does life change into fate? At death? But that is a fate *for others*, for history and for one's family. Through consciousness? But it is the mind that creates an image of life as fate, that introduces a coherence where there is none. In both cases, it is an illusion. Conclusion?: there is no fate?

Excessive use of Eurydice[7] in the literature of the forties. Because never have so many lovers been separated.

The whole art of Kafka consists in forcing the reader to reread.[8] His endings—or his absence of endings—suggest explanations which, however, do not appear clearly and require the story to be reread from another point of view to seem justified. Sometimes there is a double or triple possibility of interpretation, whence the necessity for two or three readings. But it would be wrong to try to interpret everything in Kafka in detail. A symbol is always general and the artist gives a wholesale translation of it. There is no literal application. Only the rhythm matters. And as for the rest, one must allow for chance, which is great in any creator.

[7] See *The Plague*, first chapter of IV.
[8] See Camus's article on Kafka published as an Appendix to *The Myth of Sisyphus* (Alfred A. Knopf, 1955).

In this region where winter has suppressed all color (everything is white), the least sound (the snow smothers it), all scents (the cold covers them), the first scent of growing things in the spring must be like the joyous call, the trumpet blast of sensation.

Illness is a convent which has its rule, its austerity, its silences, and its inspirations.

Algerian nights, the barkings of dogs reverberate through spaces ten times greater than in Europe. Thus the sound takes on a nostalgia unknown in these narrow regions. It is a language that I am the only one to hear today—thanks to memory.

Development of the absurd:
  1) if the basic concern is the need for unity;
  2) if the world (or God) cannot suffice.
It is up to man to forge a unity for himself, either by turning away from the world, or within the world. Thus are restored a morality and an austerity that remain to be defined.

Living with one's passions amounts to living with one's sufferings, which are the counterpoise, the corrective, the balance, and the price. When a man has learned—and not on paper—how to remain alone with his suffering, how to overcome his longing to flee, the illusion that others may share, then he has little left to learn.

Let's suppose a philosopher who after having published several works declares in a new book: "Up to now I was going in the wrong direction. I am going to begin all over. I think now that I was wrong." No one would take him seriously any more. And yet he would then be giving proof that he is worthy of thought.

Outside of love, woman is boring. She doesn't know. You must live with one and keep silent. Or else sleep with all and make love. What matters is something else.

Pascal: Error comes from exclusion.

Balance in *Macbeth:* "Fair is foul and foul is fair," but this is of diabolical origin. "And nothing is but what is not." And elsewhere, Act II, Scene 3: "For from this instant there's nothing serious in mortality." Garnier translates "The night is long that never finds the day" by "Il n'est si longue nuit qui n'atteigne le jour." (?)
Yes.[9] "It is a tale told by an idiot, full of sound and fury, signifying nothing."

The gods granted man great and dazzling virtues that put him in a position to overcome all. But at the same time they granted him a bitterer virtue which makes him scorn afterward everything that can be overcome.
. . . Constant enjoyment is impossible; weariness comes in the end. Perfect. But why? In reality one cannot always

[9] In the manuscript this word might be *Oui,* or simply *M,* in which case it would stand for Macbeth, who speaks this line.

enjoy because one cannot enjoy everything. One feels as much weariness counting up the number of enjoyments that one will never have, whatever one does, as calculating those one has already had. If one could embrace everything, in fact, really, would there be weariness?

Question to be asked: Do you love ideas—passionately, with your life? Does this thought keep you from sleeping? Do you feel that you are risking your life on it? How many philosophers would retreat!

In publishing the plays: Caligula: *tragedy;* The Exile (or Budejovice): *comedy.*

DECEMBER 15

Accept the test; extract its unity. If the opponent does not reply, die in diversity.

Beauty, Nietzsche says after Stendhal, is a promise of happiness. But if it is not happiness itself, what can it promise?

. . . It was when everything was covered with snow that I perceived that the doors and windows were blue.

If it is true that crime exhausts all man's faculty for life (see above[1]) . . . This is the way in which Cain's crime

[1] Page 17 of this *Notebook.*

(and not Adam's, which in comparison seems a venial sin) exhausted our strength and our love of life. To the extent to which we share in his nature and his condemnation, we suffer from that strange abeyance and that melancholy lack of adaptation that follow too great outbursts and exhausting deeds. At a single stroke Cain emptied for us every possibility of an effective life. That's the meaning of hell. But obviously it is on earth.

The *Princesse de Clèves*.[2] Not so simple as that. It develops by means of several tales. It starts out in complexity even though it ends in unity. In comparison with *Adolphe*, it is a complicated thriller.[3]

Its real simplicity lies in its conceptions of love: for Mme de La Fayette love is a danger. That is her postulate. And one feels throughout her book, as one does in *La Princesse de Montpensier* or *La Comtesse de Tende*, a consistent fear of love (which, by the way, is the contrary of indifference).

"His pardon was brought him as he was awaiting the final stroke of death; but fear had gripped him to such an extent that he had lost consciousness and died a few days later." (*All* the characters of La Fayette who die, die of emotion. It is easy to understand why emotion inspires such a fear in her.)

"I told her that so long as his affliction had limits I had approved it and shared it; but that I should cease to pity him if he yielded to despair and lost his reason." Magnificent. That is the reticence of our classic age. It is virile.

---

[2] See "L'Intelligence et l'échafaud," published in *Confluences* in July 1943 and reprinted in the Pléiade volume of Camus, p. 1887.
[3] Both the seventeenth-century novel by Mme de La Fayette and *Adolphe*, Benjamin Constant's psychological novel of the Romantic period, analyze love.

But it is not unfeeling. For the same man (the Prince de Clèves) who says that, later dies of despair.

"The Chevalier de Guise . . . resolved never to think again of being loved by Mme de Clèves. But in order to forsake that undertaking that had seemed to him so difficult and so glorious, he needed another great enough to keep him busy. He conceived the idea of conquering Rhodes."

"What Mme de Clèves had said of his portrait had restored him to life by revealing to him that he was the one she did not hate." The very word burns her lips.

Poverty is a state of which the virtue is generosity.

Poor childhood. Essential difference when I would go to my uncle's:[4] at home objects had no name; we used to say: the deep plates, the pot on the mantle, etc. In his house: the glazed earthenware from the Vosges, the Quimper dinner service, etc.—I awakened to the possibility of choice.

Brute physical desire is easy. But desire at the same time as affection calls for time. One has to travel through the whole land of love before finding the flame of desire. Is that why it is always so hard to desire, in the beginning, what one loves?

Essay on revolt.[5] Nostalgia for "beginnings." *Id.* The theme of the relative—but the *relative with passion.* Ex.: Torn between the world that does not suffice and God

4 Camus's uncle, M. Acault, was a butcher with a passion for literature and ideas. In the *Hommage à André Gide* of the N.R.F. (November 1951), Camus tells how this uncle lent him the first Gide he read.

5 See "Remarques sur la Révolte" in *L'Existence* (1945), which prefigures the first chapter of *The Rebel.*

who is lacking, the absurd mind passionately chooses the world. *Id.*: Divided between the relative and the absolute, it leaps eagerly into the relative.

Now that he knows its value, he is deprived. The condition of possession is ignorance. Even on the physical plane: one really possesses only a stranger.

Budejovice (or *The Exile*)

I

The mother: "No, not tonight. Let's leave him this time and this pause. Let's allow him that latitude. Perhaps it's within that latitude that we can be saved."
The daughter: "What do you mean by be saved?"
The mother: "Receive eternal forgiveness."
The daughter: "Then I am already saved. For everything to come I forgave myself in advance."

II

Id. See above.
Sister: "In the name of what?"
The wife: "In the name of my love."
Sister: "What does that word mean?"
(Pause)
Wife: "Love is my past joy and my present sorrow."
Sister: "Decidedly you are speaking a language I don't understand. Love, joy, and sorrow—I have never heard those words."

III

"Ah!" he said before dying, "so this world is not made for me and this house is not mine."

46

The sister: "The world is made to die in and a house to sleep in."

IV

Second Act. Meditation on hotel rooms. He rings. Silence. Footsteps. The old mute appears. For a moment motionless and silent outside the door.

"Nothing," he says. "Nothing. I wanted to know if someone would answer, if the bell worked."

The old man motionless a moment; then he goes away. Footsteps.

V

The sister: "Pray God to make you like a stone. That is true happiness and that is what he chose for himself.

"He is deaf, I tell you, and dumb as a piece of granite. Make yourself like him until you know nothing of the world but the trickling water and the warming sun. Join the stone while there is still time." (To be expanded.)

The absurd world can receive only an aesthetic justification.

Nietzsche: Nothing decisive is ever built except on a "despite everything."

The metaphysical novels of Maurice Blanchot[6]

Thomas l'Obscur. What attracts Anne in Thomas is the death he bears in him. Her love is metaphysical. Therefore

[6] Maurice Blanchot (1907–   ) is the author of at least five other novels of the inexplicable, in addition to the first two mentioned here, and of several stimulating essays, including one on Lautréamont and Sade.

she separates from him at the moment of dying. For at that moment she *knows* and one loves though not knowing. Hence, only death is true knowledge. But at the same time it is what makes knowledge useless: its progress is sterile.

Thomas discovers the death in him that prefigures his future. The key of the book is given in Chapter XIV. Then one has to reread and everything lights up, but with the muted light that bathes the asphodels of the realm of the dead. (Near the farm, an odd tree, made up of two interlocked trunks, one of which, long dead and with rotten base, does not even touch the ground any more. It has remained clinging to the other one and the two together symbolize Thomas rather well. But the live trunk has not let itself be strangled. It has thickened its bark's grip around the dead trunk; it has sent its branches out around and above; it has not let itself be dragged down.)

Aminadab, despite appearances, is more obscure. It's a new form of the myth of Orpheus and Eurydice (worth noting that in both books the impression of fatigue the character seems to feel and communicates to the reader is an *impression of art*).

Plague. Second version

Bible—Deuteronomy 28:21, 32:24; Leviticus 26:25; Amos 4:10; Exodus 9:4, 15; 12:29; Jeremiah 24:10, 14:12, 6:19, 21:7 and 9; Ezechiel 5:12, 6:12, 7:15.

"Each man seeks out his desert and as soon as it is found recognizes it to be too harsh. It shall not be said that I cannot endure mine."

Originally[7] the first three parts, composed of newspapers, notebooks, notations, sermons, treatises, and objective nar-

----

[7] At this point, the manuscript reads: "See Notebook"—where the following paragraph was found among the notes for *The Plague*.

ration, were to suggest, intrigue, and open up the depths of the book. The last part, composed solely of events, was to translate the general significance through them and through them alone.

Each part was also to tighten the links between the characters a little more—and was to make the significance felt by the progressive fusion of the diaries into a single diary and to complete this in the scenes of the fourth part.

Second version

The picturesque and descriptive *Plague*—little bits of documentation and a disquisition on scourges.

Stephan[8]—Chapter 2: He curses that love that cheated him of all the rest.

Put everything in the indirect style (sermons, newspapers, etc.) and monotonous relief through pictures of the Plague?

Decidedly it must be a narrative, a chronicle. But how many problems that raises.

Perhaps: reconstruct Stephan altogether by suppressing theme of love. Stephan doesn't develop. What came after suggested a broader development.

Carry along to the end the theme of separation.

Have a general report written on the plague in O.?

Those who discover a flea on them.

A chapter on poverty.

For the sermon: "Have you noticed, brethren, how monotonous Jeremiah is?"

Additional character: a man exiled from loved ones, an exile who does everything to get out of the city and cannot. His official steps: he tries to get a pass on the grounds "that he doesn't belong here." If he dies, show that he

[8] Stephan figures as a character in the first version of *The Plague*.

suffers first from not having gone back to his beloved, and from so many things left hanging. That would be the very essence of the horror of the plague.

Be careful: asthma does not justify such frequent visits.

Introduce the atmosphere of Oran.

Nothing "grimacing," just what is natural.

Civilian heroism.

Develop the social criticism and the revolt. What they lack is imagination. They settle down in an epic as in a picnic. They do not think of the scale of scourges. And the remedies they imagine are scarcely worthy of a head cold. They will perish (to be expanded).

A chapter on illness. "They noted once more that physical suffering never came to them in isolation but was always accompanied by moral sufferings (family and loves frustrated) which deepened their pain. They thus became aware—contrary to the current opinion—that if one of the painful privileges of the human lot was to die alone, it was no less cruel and no less true an image that it was never possible for man to die truly alone."

Moral of the plague: it was of no use to anything or anyone. Only those who were touched by death directly or in their families learned something. But the truth they have arrived at concerns only themselves. It has no future.

The events and the chronicles are to give the social meaning of the Plague. The characters give its deeper meaning. But all this in a general way.

Social criticism. The encounter between the administration, which is an abstract entity, and the plague, which is the most concrete of all forces, can only produce comic and scandalous results.

The man who is separated from his beloved escapes because *he cannot wait until she has grown old.*

A chapter on the relatives separated *in camps.*

End of the first part. The progression in cases of plague must be based on that of the rats. Broaden. Broaden.

The phony plague?

The first part is devoted to exposition, which ought to be altogether very rapid—even in the newspapers.

One of the possible themes: battle between medicine and religion: the powers of the relative (and what a relative!) against those of the absolute. It is the relative that wins out or rather does not lose.

"Of course, we know that the plague has its good side, that it opens eyes, that it forces us to think. In this regard it is like all the evils of this world and the world itself. But what is true likewise of the evils of this world and of the world itself is true likewise of the plague. Whatever nobility individuals derive from it, if we consider the unhappiness of our brothers, a man must be a madman, a criminal, or a coward to consent to the plague, and the only possible stance of a man when faced with it is revolt."

All seek peace. Bring this out.

?Take Cottard *in reverse:* describe his behavior and reveal *at the end* that he was afraid of being arrested.

The newspapers have nothing else to report but stories of the plague. People say: there's nothing in the newspaper.

Doctors are brought in from the outside.

What seems to me to characterize that period best is *separation.* All were separated from the rest of the world, from those they loved or from their routine. And in that withdrawal they were obliged, those who could, to meditate, and the others to live the life of hunted animals. In short, there was no alternative.

The exile, at the end, infected with the plague, runs to

a high place and calls to his wife with great shouts over the walls of the city, the countryside, three villages, and a river.

?A preface by the narrator with considerations on objectivity and eyewitness accounts.

At the end of the plague, all the inhabitants look like immigrants.

Add details of "epidemic."

Tarrou is the man who can understand everything—and who suffers thereby. He cannot judge anything.

What is the ideal of the man who is a prey to the plague? I'm certainly going to make you laugh: it's honesty.

Suppress: "in the beginning"—in fact—in reality—the first days—about at the same time, etc.

?Show throughout the book that Rieux is the narrator by a detective's means. In the beginning: cigarette smell.

At one and the same time shyness and need of warmth. To reconcile them: the movies, where one sits tight together without knowing one another.

Islands of light in the darkened city toward which a horde of shadows are converging like a mass of paramecia attracted by a heliotropism.

For the exile: evening in cafés where the lights are turned on as late as possible to save electricity, where twilight seeps into the room like gray water, the colors of the sunset being dimly reflected in the windows, the marble-topped tables and the backs of chairs shining feebly: that is the hour of his surrender.

The people suffering from separation, second part: "They were struck by the number of little things that counted greatly for them and had no existence for others. Thus they discovered personal life." "They were well aware that it had to come to an end—or at least that they ought to long for the end—and consequently they longed for it, but without the original enthusiasm—just with the very clear reasons they now had. Of the great original enthusiasm they retained only a dull dejection that made them forget the very cause of that consternation. They had the external appearance of melancholy and misfortune, but they had ceased to feel their goad. Basically, that was just what their misfortune was. Before, they were merely a prey to despair. Thus it is that many were not faithful. For from their suffering in love they had kept only a liking and a need for love and, drifting away from the creature who had awakened that liking and that need, they had felt weaker and had eventually yielded to the first promise of affection. Hence they were unfaithful through love." "Seen at a distance, their life now seemed to them to form a unit. Then it was that they clung to it with new vigor. Thus the plague restored unity to them. It must be concluded that those men were unable to live with their unity, whatever it was—or rather that they were capable of living it only when deprived of it." — "They sometimes perceived that they had stopped at the first phase, when they planned to display some day a certain thing to a certain friend who was no longer there. They still had hope. The second phase really began when they could no longer think except in terms of the plague." — "But sometimes in the middle of the night their wound would open afresh. And, suddenly awakened, they would finger its painful edges, they would recover their suffering anew and with it the stricken face of their love."

I want to express by means of the plague the stifling air from which we all suffered and the atmosphere of threat and exile in which we lived. I want at the same time to extend that interpretation to the notion of existence in general. The plague will give the image of those who in this war were limited to reflection, to silence—and to moral anguish.

Thirst is not known here and that sensation of being dried out that seizes the whole being after running in the sun and the dust. The lemonade you swallow: you don't feel the liquid going down at all but only the myriad needle pricks of the carbonation.

Not made for dispersion.

JANUARY 15

Illness is a cross, but perhaps also a guardrail. The ideal, however, would be to draw strength from it and to refuse its weaknesses. Let it be the retreat that makes one stronger *at the proper moment.* And if one has to pay in suffering and renunciation, let's pay up.

Because the sky is blue, the trees covered with snow on the edge of the stream which stretch out their white branches very low above the icy water look like almond trees in blossom. In this region the eyes are constantly confused between spring and winter.

I have started an affair with this region, in other words I have reasons for loving it and reasons for hating it. For Algeria on the other hand I have unbridled passion and I surrender to the pleasure of loving. Question: Can one love a country like a woman?

Plague—second version. Separation.

The separated people perceive that in reality they have never ceased, in the first phase, hoping for something: that letters would arrive, that the plague would end, that the absent one would slip into the city. It's only in the second phase that they no longer hope. But at that moment they have happily lost their vital energy (or else life gives them new subjects of interest). They must die or betray.

Id.: those moments when they let themselves sink into the plague and long for the relaxation it provides. Cottard says: it must be good in prison. And the inhabitants: the plague perhaps frees from everything.

Kierkegaard's purity of heart—What verbiage. Is genius therefore so slow?

"Despair is the frontier on which there come together in equal powerlessness the outburst of a cowardly timid selfishness and the temerity of a proudly obdurate mind."

"When the unclean spirit is gone out of a man, he walketh through dry places, seeking rest, and findeth none." (Matt. 12:43)

His distinction between men of action and men of suffering.

Id. for Kafka: "Terrestrial hope must be struck dead; only then can one save oneself through true hope."

Purity of heart for K. is unity. But it is unity *and* the good. There is no purity outside of God. Conclusion: resign oneself to the impure? I am far from the good and I thirst for unity. That is irreparable.

Essay on Revolt. After having placed the origin of philosophy in anguish: have it originate in happiness.

Id. To regenerate love in the absurd world amounts in fact to regenerating the most burning and most perishable of human feelings (Plato: "If we were gods, we should not know love"). But there is no value judgment to be made as to lasting love (on this earth) and the love that is not lasting. A faithful love—*if it does not wear out*—is a way for man to maintain as long as possible the best of himself. This is how fidelity is given a new value. But such a love lies outside the eternal. It is the most human of feelings with all the limitation and exaltation that the word involves. This is why man realizes himself only in love because he finds there in a dazzling form the image of his condition without future (and not, as the idealists say, because he approaches a certain form of the eternal). The type: Heathcliff. All this illustrates the fact that absurdity finds its expression in the opposition between *what lasts* and *what does not last*. Granting that there is but one way of lasting, which is lasting eternally, and that there is no middle way. We belong to the world that does not last. And all that does not last—and nothing but what does not last—is ours. Thus it is a matter of rescuing love from eternity or at least from those who dress it up in the image of eternity. I readily see the objection: obviously you have never loved. Let's drop it.

Plague. Second version.

The people who are separated lose all critical sense. The most intelligent among them can be seen looking in the newspapers and radio broadcasts for reasons for believing in a sudden end of the plague, building up unfounded hopes and feeling gratuitous fears on reading the reflections that a journalist wrote rather at random as he yawned with boredom.

The thing that lights up the world and makes it bearable is the customary feeling we have of our connections with it—and more particularly of what links us to human beings. Relations with other people always help us to carry on because they always suppose developments, a future—and also because we live as if our only purpose were to have relations with human beings. But the days when we become aware that this is not our only purpose, when we realize that our will alone keeps those human beings attached to us (stop writing or speaking, isolate yourself, and you will see them melt around you), that in reality most of them have their backs turned (not through malice, but through indifference) and that the remainder *always* have the possibility of becoming interested in something else, when we imagine in this way the element of contingency, of play of circumstances, that enters into what is called a love or a friendship, then the world returns to its night and we to that great cold whence human affection drew us for a moment.

FEBRUARY 10

Four months of ascetic and solitary life. The will, the mind profit from it. But the heart?

The whole problem of the absurd ought to be able to be centered on a critique of the value judgment and the factual judgment.

Strange text in Genesis (3:22): "And the Lord God said, Behold, the man is become as *one of us*, to know good and evil: and now, lest he put forth his hand, and take also of the tree of life, and eat, and *live for ever.*" . . .

And the flaming sword driving the man out of Eden which "turned every way, to keep the way of the tree of life." It's the story of Zeus and Prometheus all over again. Man had the power of becoming God's equal, and God feared him and kept him in bondage. *Id.* Concerning the divine responsibility.

What bothers me in the exercise of thought or the discipline necessary to the work of art is imagination. I have an unbridled imagination, without proportion, somewhat monstrous. Hard to know the tremendous role it played in my life. And yet I never noticed that personal peculiarity until the age of thirty.

Occasionally on a train or a bus the time drags and I keep myself from getting lost in playing with images or constructions that seem to me sterile. Tired of having constantly to call my thought to order, to bring it back to what I need it to feed on, there comes a moment when I let myself go, flow would be more correct: the hours rush by and I reach my destination before I am aware.

Perhaps it is my liking for stone that attracts me s much to sculpture. It restores to the human form the weight and indifference without which I cannot see any greatness in it.

Essay: a chapter on the "fecundity of tautologies."

A mind somewhat accustomed to the gymnastics of intelligence knows, like Pascal, that all error comes from an exclusion. On the frontiers of intelligence we know most certainly that there is truth in any theory and that none of the great experiences of humanity, even if they are apparently quite opposed, even if they are named Socrates and Empedocles or Pascal and Sade, is *a priori* insignificant. But the occasion forces us to a choice. In this way it seems essential to Nietzsche to attack Socrates and Christianity with forceful arguments. But in this way on the other hand it is essential for us to defend Socrates today, or at least what he represents, because the era threatens to put in their place values that are the negation of all culture and because Nietzsche might here achieve a victory that he would not want.

This seems to introduce a certain opportunism into the life of ideas. But it only seems so, for neither Nietzsche nor we lose sight of the *other side* of the question and it is merely a matter of a defense reaction. And finally Nietzsche's experience added to ours, like Pascal's added to Darwin's, Callicles's added to Plato's, restores the whole human register and returns us to our native land. (But all this can be true only with a dozen additional reservations.)

See in any case Nietzsche (*Origin of Philosophy—* Bianquis, p. 208[9]): "Socrates, I must confess, is so close to me that I am almost constantly fighting him."

Plague, second version. The people separated from others have difficulties with the days of the week. Sunday, of

[9] See Geneviève Bianquis's *Nietzsche,* published in Paris in 1933.

course. Saturday afternoon. And certain days formerly devoted to certain rites.

Id. A chapter on the terror: "People they came after at night . . ."

In the chapter on the isolation camps: the relatives are already separated from the dead—then for sanitary reasons children are separated from their parents and the men from the women. So that *separation becomes general.* All are forced into solitude.

In this way make the theme of separation the big theme of the novel. "They had asked nothing of the plague. In the center of an incomprehensible world they had patiently constructed a universe of their own, very human, in which affection and habit shared their days. And now probably it was not enough to be separated from the world itself; the plague still had to separate them from their modest daily creations. After having blinded their minds, it tore out their hearts." In practice, *there are nothing but solitary people in the novel.*

Plague, second version.

One looks for peace and turns to human beings to get it from them. But they can give nothing to begin with but madness and confusion. It must be sought elsewhere, yet the heavens are mute. And then, but only then, can one return to human beings, since, lacking peace, they give you sleep.

Plague, second version.

It is good that there are terraces above the plague.

They are *all* right, says Rieux.

Tarrou (or Rieux) forgives the plague.

Essay on Revolt. The absurd world *in the beginning* is not analyzed rigorously. It is evoked and it is imagined. Hence that world is the product of *thought in general,* in other words of precise imagination. It is the application to the conduct of life and to aesthetics of a certain modern principle. It is not an analysis.

But once that world is sketched out, the first stone (there is only one) put in place, philosophizing becomes possible—or rather, if you have fully understood—becomes necessary. Analysis and rigor are required and brought back in. Detail and description win out. From "nothing is interesting but . . ." one extracts "everything is interesting except . . ." Whence a precise and rigorous study—without conclusions—on revolt.

1) the impulse to revolt and external revolt;

2) the state of revolt;

3) metaphysical revolt.

Impulse to revolt: One's right—the feeling that it has gone on too long—that the opponent is overstepping his right (one's father, for instance). "So far, yes, but no farther"—continue the analysis.

See notes *Origin of Philosophy* and *Man of Resentment*[1] in Essay.

Essay on Revolt: one of the directions of the absurd spirit is poverty and destitution.

One way not to let oneself be "possessed" by the absurd is not to draw any advantage from it. No sexual dispersion without chastity, etc.

Id. Introduce theme of oscillation.

Id. Contemplation as one of the absurd aims, insofar as it benefits without taking sides.

1 *Vom Umsturz der Werte* by Max Scheler was translated into French in 1933 as *L'Homme du Ressentiment.*

Let's imagine a thinker who says: "There, I know that is true. But in the end I dislike the consequences and I withdraw. *Truth is unacceptable even to the one who finds it.*" This represents the absurd thinker and his constant discomfort.

This strange wind that always blows on the edge of the woods. Odd ideal of man: in the very heart of nature, to build himself a dwelling.

One must make up one's mind to introduce into matters of thought the necessary distinction between a philosophy of evidence and a philosophy of preference. In other words, one can end up with a philosophy distasteful to the mind and the heart *but which commands respect.* Thus my philosophy of evidence is the absurd. But that doesn't keep me from having (or more precisely from *knowing*) a philosophy of preference. Ex.: a fair balance between the mind and the world, harmony, plenitude, etc. . . . The happy thinker is the one who follows his inclination; the exiled thinker is the one who refuses to do so—out of truth—with regret but determination . . .

Can one push as far as possible such a separation between the thinker and his system? Isn't it in fact returning to an indirect realism?—truth external to the man and constraining. Perhaps, but it would then be an unsatisfactory realism. Not an *a priori* solution.

The great problem to be solved "practically": can one be happy and solitary?

Anthology of insignificance.[2] And first of all, what is insignificance? Here the etymology is misleading. It is not what has no meaning. For then it would have to be said that the world is insignificant. Senseless and insignificant are not synonymous. An insignificant character can be quite reasonable. It is not what is futile either. There are great deeds, serious and grandiose projects that are insignificant. This, however, puts us on the track. For those deeds do not seem insignificant to whoever undertakes them with official seriousness. One must consequently add that they are insignificant for . . . that a character is insignificant in regard to . . . that a thought is insignificant in relation to . . . In other words, and it applies to everything, there is a relativity of insignificance. Which does not mean that insignificance is a relative thing. It bears relation to something that is not insignificance—that has meaning—a certain importance, that "counts," that deserves interest, that is worth pausing over, paying attention to, devoting oneself to, that has a place and justly so, that strikes the mind, that calls attention to itself, that is flagrantly obvious, etc. That thing is not yet any easier to define. Insignificance will be relative only if several definitions can be given of this standard of significance. Otherwise it is, like everything else, comparable to something greater, deriving the little meaning it has from a more general significance. Let us pause over these words. To a certain degree, with great precaution and calling to the rescue numerous reservations, it might be said that an insignificant thing is not necessarily a thing that has no *meaning*, but a thing that has not, in itself, a general *significance*. In other words, and according to the normal scale of values, if I get married I perform an act that

[2] See "De l'insignificance" by Camus in *Cahiers des Saisons* (1959), reprinted in the Pléiade volume of Camus, p. 1894.

takes on a general significance in the order of the species, another in the order of society, in that of religion, and perhaps a final one in the metaphysical order. Conclusion: marriage is not an insignificant act, at least in the order of commonly accepted values. For if the significance of the species, of society, or of religion is taken from it, as it would be for all who are indifferent to such considerations, marriage is really an insignificant act. However that may be, on the basis of that example it is evident that insignificance depends on the significance it lacks.

To take a contrary example, if to open a door I turn the latch toward the right instead of toward the left, I cannot relate that gesture to any commonly accepted general significance. Society, religion, the species, and God himself don't give a damn whether I turn the latch to the right or to the left. Conclusion: my act is insignificant, unless for me that habit is related for instance to an anxiety to save my strength, to a liking for efficiency that may reflect a certain will, a manner of life, etc. In which case it will be much more important for me to turn my latch in a certain way than to get married. Hence significance always has its relationship which determines what it is. The general conclusion is that there is uncertainty in the case of insignificance.

But as I am planning to make an anthology of insignificant acts, I therefore know what an insignificant act is. Probably. But knowing whether or not an act is insignificant is not in itself knowing what insignificance is. And, after all, I can for example make that anthology to get to the bottom of the problem. Meanwhile . . .

Outline.

1) Insignificant acts: the old man and the cat[3]—the

3 See *The Plague*, third chapter of I.

soldier and the girl[4] (Note for this one. I hesitated to place
this story in the anthology. Perhaps it has a great significance. But I include it nevertheless to show the great difficulty of my undertaking. In any case, it will be possible
to include it *also* in an anthology of things that have meaning—in preparation), etc., etc.

2) Insignificant words. "As they say in my region" —
"As Napoleon used to say" — and, in a general way, most
historical remarks. Jarry's toothpick.[5]

3) Insignificant thoughts. Several huge volumes will be
needed.

Why such an anthology? It is worth noticing that eventually insignificance is almost always identified with the
mechanical aspect of things and persons—with habit most
often. In other words, everything eventually becoming
habitual, one can be sure that the greatest thoughts and
the greatest deeds eventually become insignificant. Life
has as its predestined aim insignificance. Whence the
interest of the anthology. It describes practically not only
the largest part of existence (that of little acts, tiny
thoughts, and passing moods) but also our common future.
It has the extremely rare advantage today of being truly
prophetic.

Nietzsche, with the most monotonous external life possible, proves that thought alone, carried on in solitude, is a
frightening adventure.

4 See *Notebooks, 1935–1942*, p. 178.
5 For an earlier reference to Jarry's toothpick, see *Notebooks, 1935–
1942*, p. 146.

We endure the fact that Molière had to die!

March 9. The first periwinkles—and it was snowing a week ago!

Nietzsche knows nostalgia also. But he will not ask anything of heaven. His solution: what one cannot ask of God one asks of man: this is the superman. Amazing that to avenge such pretension he was not made a God himself. Perhaps it's merely a matter of patience. Buddha preaches a wisdom without gods and a few centuries later he is put on an altar.

The European who turns courage into a personal pleasure: he admires himself. Repulsive. True courage is passive: it is indifference to death. An ideal: pure knowledge and happiness.

What better can a man wish for than poverty? I didn't say destitution nor yet the hopeless labor of the modern proletariat. But I don't see what anyone can want more than poverty with the possibility of activity in leisure.

Value judgments cannot be suppressed *absolutely*. That negates the absurd.

The ancient philosophers (quite understandably) meditated more than they read. That is why they clung so closely to the concrete. Printing changed all that. We read more than we meditate. We have no philosophies but merely commentaries. This is what Gilson says, considering that the age of philosophers concerned with philosophy was followed by the age of professors of philosophy concerned with philosophers. Such an attitude shows both modesty and impotence. And a thinker who began his book with these words: "Let us take things from the beginning," would evoke smiles. It has come to the point where a book of philosophy appearing today without basing itself on any authority, quotation, or commentary would not be taken seriously. And yet . . .

For *The Plague:* There are more things in men to admire than to despise.

When one chooses renunciation despite the certainty that "everything is permitted," something remains nonetheless—one ceases to judge others.

What attracts many people to the novel is that apparently it's a form without a style. In fact it requires the most difficult style, one that subjects itself altogether to the object. Hence it is possible to imagine an author writing each of his novels in a different style.

The sensation of death that is henceforth familiar to me; it is deprived of the aid of pain. Pain clings to the present; it calls for a struggle that *keeps one busy*. But foreseeing death from the mere sight of a handkerchief filled with blood is being plunged suddenly and effortlessly into time in a dizzying way: it is the fear of what's ahead.

The thickness of the clouds decreased. As soon as the sun could come out, the ploughed fields began to steam.

Death gives its shape to love as it does to life—transforming it into fate. The one you love died while you loved her and now it is a love fixed forever—which, without such an end, would have fallen to pieces. What would the world be without death—a succession of forms evaporating and returning, an anguished flight, an unfinishable world. But fortunately here is death, the stable one. And the lover weeping over the beloved's remains, René beside Pauline, sheds the tears of pure joy—with the feeling that all is finished—of the man who finally recognizes that his fate has taken shape.

The odd theory of Mme de La Fayette is that of marriage considered as the lesser of two evils. It is better to have made a bad marriage than to suffer from passion. There can be seen an ethic of *Order*.

(The French novel is psychological because it is suspicious of metaphysics. It constantly refers to the human out of *prudence*.) Only a careless reading of *La Princesse de Clèves* could draw from it the image of the classical novel. It is very poorly composed, on the contrary.

Plague. The separated people: Journal of the Separation? "The feeling of separation was general and it is possible to give an idea of it from conversations, confidences, and the news in the papers."

Id. The separated people. That evening hour which, for

believers, is the hour of self-scrutiny, is hard on the prisoner—it is the hour of frustrated love.

Plague. *Id.* Hunger forces some to meditation and others
to go after supplies. Consequently, not only what brought
misfortune was at the same time a good, but what was a
misfortune for some was a good for others. One couldn't
disentangle it.

?Stephan. Journal of separation.

Three levels in the work: Tarrou who describes in detail;
Stephan who calls forth *the general;* Rieux who reconciles
them in the higher conversion of the *relative diagnosis.*

The separated people. *Id.* At the very end of the time of
the plague, they ceased to imagine that intimacy that
had been theirs and how there could live beside them a
person on whom they could lay their hand at any moment.

Epigraph for *The Misunderstanding?* "What is born does
not tend to perfection and yet never stops"—Montaigne.[6]

It is easy to imagine a European converted to Buddhism
—because it assures him of survival—which Buddha considers an incurable misfortune, but which the European
desires with all his strength.

Saint-Étienne and its suburbs. Such a sight is the condemnation of the civilization that produced it. A world in
which there is no more place for the human being, for
joy, for active leisure, is a world that must die. No group

6 When *Le Malentendu* (earlier referred to as *Budejovice*) was published in 1944, it bore no epigraph.

of people can live devoid of beauty. They can go on living for a time and that's all. And the Europe that presents one of its most characteristic faces here is progressively getting away from beauty. That is why it is going through convulsions and that's why it will die if peace does not signify for it a return to beauty and love's return to its rightful place.

Any life directed toward money is a death. Renascence lies in disinterestedness.

In the mere fact of writing there is evidence of a personal assurance that I am beginning to lack. Assurance that one has something to say and especially that something can be said—assurance that what one feels and what one is has value as an example—assurance that one is irreplaceable and not a coward. All that is what I am losing and I am beginning to imagine the moment when I shall no longer write.

One must have the strength to choose what one prefers and to cling to it. Otherwise it's better to die.

The separated people: "They waited impatiently, in order to relive their love, for the moment of unmotivated jealousy."

Id. They are asked to sign up so as to have a list of those who are separated. They are amazed that nothing comes of it. But this is merely a way of knowing the names of those to inform "in case." "Well, we'll sign up."

Id. Third page. "But when they had found each other again, they still had considerable trouble substituting the real person for the creation of their imaginations . . . and it can be said that the plague did not die until the day when one of them could again look with boredom at the one facing him."

Every thought is judged by what it is able to draw from suffering. Despite my dislike of it, suffering is a fact.

I cannot live without beauty. That's what makes me weak in the face of certain people.

When all is finished, *step aside* (God *or* woman).

What most distinguishes man from the animal is imagination. Wherefor our experience of sex cannot be truly natural, in other words blind.

The absurd is the tragic man facing a mirror (Caligula). So he is *not alone*. There is the germ of a satisfaction or of a self-indulgence. Now the mirror must be suppressed.

Time does not go fast when one observes it. It feels watched. But it takes advantage of our distractions. Perhaps there are even two times, the one we observe and the one that transforms us.

Epigraph for *The Misunderstanding:* "This is why the poets figure that wretched mother Niobe, having first lost seven sons and subsequently as many daughters, overwhelmed with losses, and being finally transmuted into a rock . . . to express that feelingless, mute, and deaf stupidity that seizes us when accidents beyond our bearing crush us." — Montaigne.

Id. "Concerning melancholy": "I am one of the freest from that passion and neither having it nor esteeming it, although the world has begun . . . to honor it with particular favor."

Id. ("Concerning liars"): "And there is nothing that shows the strength of a horse more than coming to a sharp, clear stop."

Absurd. Restore ethics by the personal form of address. I do not believe there is another world in which we shall have to "render account." But we already have our account to render in this world—to all those we love.

Id. On the subject of speech (Parain: the arguments proving that man could not have invented speech are irrefutable.) Everything, the moment one gets beneath the surface, leads to a metaphysical problem. Consequently, everywhere man turns he is isolated on reality as if he were on an island surrounded by a noisy sea of possibles and interrogations. One cannot draw the conclusion that the world has meaning. For it would have none if it were just that, crudely. Happy worlds give rise to no reasons. Hence it is ridiculous to say: "Is metaphysics possible?" Metaphysics *is*.

The consolation of this world is that there are no continuous sufferings. A pain disappears and a joy is reborn. All balances out. This world is counterbalanced. And if even our will extracts from the future a privileged suffering that we raise to the level of a force in order to feel it constantly, there is in that choice a proof that we consider such suffering as a good and there, this time, compensation resides.

Third of *Thoughts Out of Season:*[7] "With a painful look in his eye, Schopenhauer turned away from the portrait of Rancé, the founder of the Trappist Order, saying: 'This calls for grace.' "

Regarding M. I don't refuse a path leading to the Supreme Being, so long as it doesn't avoid other beings. To know if one can find God as the outcome of one's passions.

Plague: most important. "It is because they gave you the problem of food supply and the pain of separations that they had you without revolt."

[7] Camus read in French Nietzsche's *Unzeitgemässe Betrachtungen*.

73

MAY 20

For the first time: strange feeling of satisfaction and of fulfillment. Question I asked myself, lying in the grass, facing the heavy, warm evening: "If these days were the last ..." Reply: a calm smile in me. Yet nothing I can be proud of: nothing is solved; my very conduct is not clearly defined. Is this the hardening at the end of an experiment, or the soft influence of the evening, or on the other hand the beginning of a wisdom that has ceased to negate anything?

JUNE. LUXEMBOURG GARDENS

A Sunday morning full of wind and sunlight. Over the large pool the wind splatters the waters of the fountain; the tiny sailboats on the windswept water and the swallows around the huge trees. Two youths discussing: "You who believe in human dignity."

Prologue: "Love ..."
"Knowledge ..."
"It's the same word."

Although in daylight the flights of birds always seem aimless, in the evening they always seem to have found a destination. They are flying toward something. Thus it is perhaps in the evening of life ...

Is there an evening of life?[8]

[8] This sentence was added in pencil on the manuscript.

74

Hotel room in Valence. "I don't want you to do that. What would I become with that thought? What shall I become faced with your mother, your sisters, Marie-Rolande, I had promised myself not to tell you this, you are well aware. — I beg you, don't do it. I had such a need of these two days of rest. I'll keep you from doing it. I don't care what I have to do. I'll marry you if I have to. But I can't have that on my conscience. — I had promised myself not to tell you this. — Those are just words. And acts are what matter to me . . . — People will think of an accident. The train . . . etc. (She weeps. She shouts: 'I hate you. I hate you for doing that to me.') — I'm well aware, Rolande, I'm well aware. But I didn't want to tell you, etc., etc." He promises. Time: an hour and a half. Monotony. Marking time.

Van Gogh struck by a thought of Renan: "Forget oneself; achieve great things, reach nobility and go beyond the vulgarity in which the existence of most individuals stagnates."

"If one continues loving sincerely what is truly worthy of love and *does not waste one's love on insignificant things and meaningless things and colorless things,* gradually one will get more light and become stronger."

"If one perfects oneself in a single thing and understands it fully, one achieves in addition understanding and knowledge of many other things."

"I am a faithful sort of person in my faithlessness."

"If I make landscapes, there will always be a hint of faces in them."

He quotes Doré's remark: "I have the patience of an ox." See letter 340 on the trip to Zweeloo.

The bad taste of great artists: he equates Millet with Rembrandt.

"I believe more and more that God must not be judged on the basis of this world; it's one of his rough sketches."

"I can readily, in life and in painting too, get along without God, but I cannot, when ill, get along without something that is greater than I, which is my life, the power of creation."

Van Gogh's long groping until the age of twenty-seven before finding his way and discovering that he is a painter.

When one has done everything necessary to understand, accept, and endure poverty, illness and its shortcomings, there is still a step to be taken.

Plague. Sentimental professor[9] at the end of the plague concludes that the only intelligent occupation is to copy a book backward (develop the text and the meaning).

Tarrou dies in silence (wink, etc.).

Administrative isolation camp.

Conversation at the end with professor and doctor: they are together again. But they had not asked for much. *I didn't have*, etc.

The Jewish quarter (the flies). Those who want to keep up appearances. People are invited for a cup of ersatz coffee.

Separated people. Second. And what was already so hard to endure for themselves (old age), they now had to endure for two.

Yet current affairs continue to be taken care of. It was then, indeed, that people learned the results of an affair that had aroused in its day the curiosity of those who

[9] Stephan, referred to earlier as in the first version.

go in for such things. A young murderer . . . had been
pardoned. The newspapers thought he would get off with
ten years of good conduct and could then resume his
normal life. It really wasn't worth while.

Confidence in words is classicism—but to keep its con-
dence it uses them with discretion. Surrealism, which is
suspicious of them, abuses them. Let us go back to classicism, out of modesty.

Those who love truth must look for love in marriage;
in other words, love without illusions.

"What does the inspiration of Occitania consist of?" A
special issue of *Cahiers du Sud*.[1] In brief, we were no good
during the Renaissance, the eighteenth century, and the
Revolution. We counted for something only from the tenth
century to the thirteenth and at a time when, it so happens,
it is very hard to speak of us as a nation—when all civilization is international. Hence, of whole centuries of history,
misfortune or fame, the hundred or so great names they
left us, a tradition, a national life, love—all that is empty
and worthless. And *we* are the nihilists!

Humanism doesn't bore me; it even appeals to me. But
I find it inadequate.

[1] No. 249 of *Cahiers du Sud* (August–October 1942), entitled "The
Genius of Oc and the Mediterranean Man," contained a long article by
E. Novis on the inspiration of the region of the *langue d'oc*, sometimes
known as Occitania.

Brück, a Dominican:[2] "Those Christian Democrats give me a pain in the neck."

"G. has the look of a priest, a sort of episcopal unction. And I can hardly bear it even in bishops."

I: "As a young man, I thought all priests were happy."
Brück: "Fear of losing their faith makes them limit their sensitivity. It becomes merely a negative vocation. They don't face up to life." (His dream: a great conquering clergy, but magnificent in its poverty and audacity.)
Conversation on a damned Nietzsche.

Barrès and Gide.[3] Uprooting is a problem we have gone beyond. And when problems don't interest us passionately, we indulge in less nonsense. After all, we need a native soil and we need travel.

Misunderstanding. The wife, after the husband's death: "How I love him."

Agrippa d'Aubigné:[4] There is a man who believes and who fights because he believes. After all, he is happy. This can be seen in the satisfaction he takes in his house, in his life, in his career. When he rages, he does so against those who are wrong—according to him.

[2] Father Raymond M. Bruckberger (1907–   ) has long been a figure in Parisian literary circles. His *Image of America* was published in English in 1959.
[3] Maurice Barrès, who extolled native roots, and André Gide, who praised nomadism, clashed in 1897 in an exchange of articles recorded in Gide's *Pretexts* (Meridian Books, 1959).
[4] In Camus's archives there are three pages of notes on this vigorous Protestant poet of the late sixteenth century.

What makes a tragedy is that each of the forces in opposition is equally legitimate, has a right to live. Whence a weak tragedy: which involves illegitimate forces. Whence a strong tragedy: which legitimizes *everything*.

On the plateaus of the Mézenc, the wind whistling like sweeping swords in the air.

Living with one's passions assumes that one has subjugated them.

Eternal Return assumes indulgence in pain.

Life is cluttered with events that make us long to grow older.

Do not forget: illness and decrepitude. There's not a minute to be wasted—which is perhaps the contrary of "one must hurry."

Moral: One can't live with people when knowing their ulterior motives.

Resolutely reject any collective judgment. Introduce innocence into the "commentary" aspect of any society.

Heat ripens people like fruit. They are ripe before having lived. They know everything before having learned anything.

B.B.: "Nobody realizes that some people expend tremendous energy merely to be normal."

Plague: If Tarrou's notebooks play such a part, this is because he happened to die at the narrator's (in the beginning).

"Are you sure that contagion is a fact and that isolation is desirable?" "I am not sure of anything, but I am sure that dead bodies left abandoned, promiscuity, etc., are not desirable. Theories may change, but there is something that is valid always and in all seasons: consistency."

As a result of their constant battle, the sanitation squads cease to be interested in news of the plague.

The plague suppresses value judgments. The quality of clothing, of food, etc., is no longer judged. Everything is accepted.

The separated man wants to ask the doctor for a certificate to get out (this is how he comes to know him); he tells of his official steps . . . He comes back regularly.

The trains, the stations, the waiting.

The plague emphasizes separation. But the fact of being together is merely a chance that is prolonged. The plague is the rule.

SEPTEMBER 1, 1943

He who despairs of events is a coward, but he who has hope for the human lot is a fool.

SEPTEMBER 15

He drops everything, personal work, business letters, etc., to reply to a thirteen-year-old girl who writes him from the heart!

Inasmuch as the word "existence" applies to something, which is our nostalgia, but as it cannot keep from extending to the affirmation of a higher reality, we shall keep it only in a converted form—we shall say inexistential philosophy, which does not involve a negation but aims merely to report on the state of "the man deprived of . . ." Inexistential philosophy will be the philosophy of exile.

Sade: "People decry the passions without thinking that it is their flame that lights the flame of philosophy."

Art has impulses of discretion. It cannot say things directly.

In a revolutionary period it is always the best who die. The law of sacrifice leaves the last word to the cowards and the timorous since the others have lost it by giving the best of themselves. The ability to speak always implies that one has betrayed.

Artists are the only ones who do any good in the world. No, says Parain.

Plague. All fight—and each in his way. The only cowardice is falling on one's knees . . . Many new moralists appeared and their conclusion was always the same: one must fall on one's knees. But Rieux replied: one must fight in such and such a way.

The exile spends hours in railway stations. Revitalize the dead station.

Rieux: "In any fighting group one needs men who kill and men who cure. I have chosen to cure. But I know that I am fighting."

Plague. There are at this moment distant harbors in which the water is pink in the sunset.

"Coming to God because you are detached from the earth and because pain has separated you from the world is useless. God needs souls attached to the world. It is your joy that gratifies him."

Repeating this world is perhaps betraying it more surely than by transfiguring it. The best of photographs is in itself a treason.

Against rationalism. If pure determinism has a meaning, a single true affirmation would be enough for us to arrive, through one conclusion after another, at the whole truth. But that is not so. Therefore, either we have never pronounced a single true affirmation—not even the affirmation that everything is determined. Or else we have spoken the truth but *to no effect* and determinism is false.

82

For my "creation against God."[5] It's a Catholic critic (Stanislas Fumet) who says that art, *whatever its aim,* always competes guiltily with God. Likewise, Roger Secrétain in *Cahiers du Sud,* August–September '43. And also Péguy: "There is even a poetry that takes its luster from the absence of God, that counts on no salvation, that depends on nothing but itself, human effort rewarded here on earth, to fill the void of spaces."

There is no middle path between apologetic literature and competitive literature.

One's duty is to do what one knows to be fair and good —"preferable." That is easy? No, for even what one knows to be preferable, one does with difficulty.

Absurd. If one kills oneself, the absurd is negated. If one does not kill oneself, the absurd reveals on application a principle of satisfaction that negates itself. This does not mean that the absurd does not exist. It means that the absurd is *truly* without logic. This is why one cannot *truly* live on it.

PARIS. NOVEMBER 1943[6]

Suréna.[7] In the fourth act, all the doors are guarded. And Eurydice, who up to now has struck such wonderful notes,

5 See "Revolt and Art" in *The Rebel.* Fumet and Secrétain were well known as Catholic writers; so was Charles Péguy, of an older generation.
6 On November 2, 1943, Camus became an editor of Editions Gallimard in Paris.
7 Produced in 1674, *Suréna* was Corneille's last play; it depicts the thwarted love of the Parthian general Suréna and the Armenian princess Eurydice.

begins to be silent, to search her heart without being able to express the word that would deliver her. She will keep silent until the end—when she dies through not having spoken. And Suréna:

"Ah! . . . the pain oppressing me . . .
Do not treat it as mere affection."

The wonderful feat of the classic theater, in which successive couples of actors come on to tell events without ever living them—and yet the anguish and action never cease growing.

Parain. They all cheated. They never transcended the despair that engulfed them. And that because of literature. A Communist for him is someone who has given up language and substituted for it *factual revolt*. He has chosen to do what Christ scorned doing: to save the damned—by damning himself.

There is a stage in suffering, or in any emotion, or passion, when it belongs to what is most personal and inexpressible in man and there is a stage when it belongs to art. But in its first moments art can never do anything with it. Art is the distance that time gives to suffering.

It is man's transcendence in relation to himself.

With Sade,[8] systematic eroticism is one of the directions of absurd thought.

For Kafka, death is not a deliverance. His humble pessimism, according to Magny.[9]

[8] See "A Man of Letters," in *The Rebel*.
[9] Claude-Edmonde Magny is a major French critic of modern literature.

Plague. Love had assumed in them the form of obstinacy.

Add on proofs of *Caligula:* "Well, the tragedy is over. The failure is complete. I turn my head and go away. I took my share in this fight for the impossible. Let us wait for death, knowing in advance that death liberates from nothing."[1]

"Christ died perhaps for someone, but it was not for me." Man is guilty, but he is so for not having been able to derive everything from himself—this is a mistake that has grown since the beginning.

On justice—the fellow who ceases to believe in it as soon as he is put through a rough grilling.
Id. What I blame Christianity for is being a doctrine of injustice.

Plague. End up with a motionless woman in mourning announcing in sufferings what men have given in lives and blood.

Thirty years old
Man's first faculty is forgetfulness. But it is fair to say that he forgets even the good he has done.

Plague. Separation is the rule, The rest is chance.
—but people are always brought together.
—there are chances that last a whole lifetime.

[1] In fact, Camus did not use these notes for his play.

Sea bathing is forbidden. That is an indication. It is forbidden to delight one's body; to return to the truth of things. But the plague ends and there will be a truth of things.

Diary of the separated man?

The greatest saving one can make in the order of thought is to accept the unintelligiblity of the world—and to pay attention to man.

When, in old age, one achieves a wisdom or an ethic, one must be embarrassed by regret of all one has done contrary to that ethic and that wisdom. Too much in advance or too late. There is no middle.

I frequent the X family because they have a better memory than I. They make our common past richer for me by bringing back to my mind everything that had left it.

For the work to be a challenge, it must be finished (this is why one must say "without sequel"). It is the opposite of divine creation. It is finished, thoroughly limited, clear, molded to the human requirement. The unity is in our hands.

Parain. Can the individual choose the moment when he can die for truth?

In this world, there are witnesses and spoilers. As soon as a man bears witness and dies, his testimony is messed up and spoiled by words, preachings, art, etc.

Success can improve the young man, as happiness does the mature man. Once his effort is recognized, he can add to it relaxation and unconstraint, royal virtues.

Roger Bacon spends *twelve years* in prison for having asserted the primacy of experience in matters of knowledge.

There is a moment when youth is lost. It's the moment when one loses human beings. And one must know how to accept it. But that moment is hard.

Regarding the American novel: it aims at the universal. Like classicism. But whereas classicism aims at an eternal universal, contemporary literature, as a result of circumstances (interpenetration of frontiers), aims at a historical universal. It's not the man of all times, but the man of all spaces.

Plague. "He liked to wake up at 4 a.m. and imagine her then. It was the time when he could catch hold of her. At 4 a.m., *people are doing nothing;* they are sleeping."[2]
A theatrical company is still playing: a play about Orpheus and Eurydice.[3]

[2] See Rambert in *The Plague*, 11.
[3] See *The Plague*, first chapter of IV.

The separated people: the world . . . But who am I to judge them? They all are right. But there is no way out.

Conversation on friendship between Doctor and Tarrou: "I've thought of it. But it's not possible. The plague leaves *no time*." Suddenly: "At this moment we are all living *for* death. That gives you food for thought."

Id. A fellow who chooses *silence.*

"Defend yourself," the judges said.
"No," the accused said.
"Why?" But you must."
"Not yet. I want you to take your full responsibility."

Concerning the natural in art. It is impossible in the absolute state. Because the real is impossible (bad taste, vulgarity, inappropriateness to the deeper needs of man). That is why human creation, starting out from the world, eventually turns against the world. Lurid novels are bad because for the most part they are true (either because reality has conformed to them, or because the world is conventional). Art and the artist remake the world, but always with an ulterior motive of protest.

Portrait of S. by A.: "His grace, his sensitivity, that mixture of nonchalance and firmness, of discretion and daring, that naïveté that does not keep him from being healthily on his guard."

The Greeks would not have understood anything about Existentialism—although, *despite the scandal,* they were able to become Christian. This is because Existentialism does not assume a *behavior*.

Id. There is no knowledge that is absolutely pure, in other words disinterested. Art is an attempt, through description, at pure knowledge.

Raising the question of the absurd world amounts to asking: "Are we going to accept despair, without doing anything?" I suppose that no one honest can answer yes.

Algeria. I don't know whether or not I can make myself understood, but I have the same feeling on returning to Algeria as I have on looking at the face of a child. And yet I know that all is not pure.

My work. Finish series of works on the created world: *"Creation corrected."*

If the work, a product of revolt, sums up the totality of man's aspirations, it is obligatorily idealistic. (?) Thus the purest product of rebellious creation is the novel of love which . . .

The extraordinary confusion that results in poetry being presented to us as a spiritual exercise and the novel as a personal purgation.

Novel. In the face of action or death, all the attitudes of a single man. But each time, as if the attitude were the proper one.

Plague. One cannot enjoy the cry of birds in the coolness of the evening—in the world as it is. For it is covered now with a so thick layer of history that its speech must get through to reach us. It is deformed thereby. Nothing of the world can be felt for its own sake, because a whole series of images of death and despair is bound to each of its moments. No more mornings without deaths, no more evenings without imprisonments, and no more noons without dreadful slaughter.

Memoirs of an executioner. "I alternate kindness and violence. Psychologically, it's a good thing."

Plague. The fellow who wonders whether he should join the sanitation squads or save himself for his great love. Fecundity! Where is it?

Id. After the curfew, the city is all stone.

Id. What bothered them was the insecurity. Every day, every hour, without respite, hunted down, uncertain.

Id. I try to keep myself in readiness. But there is always an hour of the day or night when a man is cowardly. That's the hour I am afraid of.

Id. The isolation camp. "I knew what it was like. I'd be forgotten, that was sure. Those who didn't know me would forget me because they would be thinking of something else and those who know me and love me would forget me because they would exhaust themselves in official steps and plans for getting me out. In any case, no one would think of me. No one would imagine me minute by minute, etc., etc."

(Have Rambert inspect them.)

Id. The sanitation squads or the men of the redemption. All the men in the sanitation squads look sad.

Id. "It was on this terrace that Dr. Rieux had the idea of leaving a chronicle of the event which would clearly bring out the solidarity he felt with those people. And that testimony which closes here . . . etc."

Id. During the plague people don't live by the body; they lose their flesh.

Id. Beginning: The doctor accompanies his wife to the station. But he is forced to demand that the city be closed.

Being and Nothingness (pp. 135–36).[4] Strange error about our lives because we try to experience our lives from the outside.

If the body feels its nostalgia for the soul, there is no reason why in eternity the soul should not suffer painfully from its separation from the body—and why it should not then long to return to earth.

One writes in moments of despair. But what is despair?

Nothing can be based on love: it is flight, anguish, wonderful moments or hasty fall. But it is not . . .

Paris or the very setting of sensitivity.

[4] This is of course the basic philosophical treatise of Sartre, *L'Être et le Néant*, first published in 1943.

Short stories. In the midst of revolution the fellow who promises safety to his adversaries. Later a tribunal of his party condemns them to death. He helps them escape.

Id. A priest under torture betrays.[5]

Id. Cyanide. He doesn't use it to see if he can stick it out to the end.

Id. The fellow who suddenly takes a part in civil defense. He nurses the wounded. But he has kept his arm band. He is shot.

Id. The coward.

Plague. *After* the plague he *hears* the rain on the ground for the first time.

Id. As he was going to die, it became urgent to consider that life was stupid. This was what he had thought up to then; let it at least be of some use in this difficult moment. After all, just at the moment when he needed any possible advantage, he wasn't going to see a smile on the face that had always been closed to him.

Id. The fellow who was hospitalized through a mistake. "It's a mistake," he said. "What mistake? Don't be stupid. There are never mistakes."

Id. Medicine and religion: two functions that seem compatible. But today, when all is clear, one realizes that they are irreconcilable, and that one must choose between the relative and the absolute. "If I believed in God, I should not treat mankind. If I had an idea that mankind could be cured, I should not believe in God."

Justice: the experience of justice *through sport.*

Plague. The fellow who accepts philosophically the illness of others. But if his best friend is ill, he does all he

5 This theme is found in "The Renegade" (*Exile and the Kingdom*).

can. Consequently solidarity in the fight is meaningless; individual feelings are what win out.

Tarrou's chronicle: a boxing match—Tarrou finds a boxing pal. Clandestine fights organized—a football—a tribunal.

That happiness in the morning when after a good breakfast one walks through the streets smoking a cigarette. There were still good moments.

Tarrou: "It's odd, but you have a sad philosophy and a happy face." Then conclude that my philosophy is not sad.

In the middle, all the characters meet in the same sanitation squad. A chapter on a big get-together.

The Sunday of a football player who can't play any more. Link him to Tarrou. Since football games are forbidden, Étienne Villaplane is bored on Sunday. What his Sundays were. What they now are: he wanders through the streets, kicking stones that he tries to shoot straight into the sewer holes ("A goal," he said, adding that life was lousy). He mingles with the children playing, whenever there's a ball involved. He spits out his cigarette butts and boosts them with a kick (in the beginning, of course; later he kept the butts).

Rieux and Tarrou.

Rieux: "When a man writes what you write, it seems that he has nothing to do with the concerns of men."

"Oh come," Tarrou said, "it only seems so."

W. Anything she can define seems contemptible to her. She says: "It's nauseating. It's just the so-called battle of the sexes." But the battle of the sexes exists and we can do nothing about it.

A person who insists that *the other* do everything and then accepts and lives passively—except for acting, energetically too, to persuade the other to continue giving all and doing all.

Essay on Revolt: "All rebels act, however, as if they believed in the completion of history. The contradiction is . . ."

Id. Only a few really want liberty. The majority want justice and the majority even confuse justice and liberty. But question: is absolute justice the equivalent of absolute happiness? One comes to the idea that it is essential to choose between sacrificing liberty to justice or justice to liberty. For an artist, this amounts in certain circumstances to choosing between one's art and the happiness of mankind.

Can man alone create his own values? That is the whole problem.

Are you pertinent? But I never said that man was not reasonable. What I want is to deprive him of his imaginary survival and show that with such privation he is at last clear and coherent.

Id. Sacrifice leading to value. But the suicide is selfish too: puts forward a value that seems to him more important than his own life—it's the feeling of that respectable and happy life of which he has been deprived.

Look upon heroism and courage as secondary values— *after having given proof of courage.*

Novel of the appointed suicide. Set for a year from now—his formidable superiority from the fact that death is a matter of indifference to him.

Link him to novel about love?

Mad nature of sacrifice: the fellow who dies for something *he will not see*.

I took ten years to win what seems to me priceless: a heart without bitterness. And as often happens, once I had gone beyond the bitterness, I incorporated it in one or two books. Thus I shall be forever judged on that bitterness which has ceased to mean anything to me. But that is just. It's the price one must pay.

The dreadful and consuming selfishness of artists.

A love can be preserved only for reasons external to love. Moral reasons, for instance.

Novel. What is love for her? — that void, that little hollow in her since they discovered each other, that call of lovers toward each other, shouting each other's name.

One cannot be capable of commitment on all planes. At least one can choose to live on the plane on which commitment is possible. Live according to what is honorable in oneself and only that. In certain cases this may lead to turning away from human beings even (and above all) when one has a passion for human beings.

In any case this constitutes a wrench. But what does

that prove? It proves that whoever *seriously* tackles the moral problem must end in extremes. Whether you are for (Pascal) or against (Nietzsche), you only have to be so seriously to see that the moral problem is nothing but blood, madness, and shouting.

Revolt. Chap. I. Ethics exists. The immoral thing is Christianity. Definition of an ethics against intellectual rationalism and divine irrationalism.

Chap. X. Conspiring as a moral value.

Novel
She who ruined everything through absentmindedness: "And yet, I loved him with all my soul."

"Well," said the priest, "it still wasn't enough."

SUNDAY, SEPTEMBER 24, 1944, LETTER
Novel: "Night of avowals, of tears and kisses. Bed damp with tears, with sweat, with love. The height of every heart-rending."

Novel. A handsome creature. And he gets everything forgiven.

Those who love all women are those who are on their way toward abstraction. They go beyond this world, however it may seem. For they turn away from the particular, from the individual case. The man who would flee all thought, all abstraction, the truly desperate one, is the man of a single woman. Through persistence in that singular face which cannot satisfy everything.

December. This heart full of tears and of night.

Plague. Separated, they write each other and he strikes the right note and keeps her love. Triumph of words and of style.

Justification of art: the true work of art helps sincerity, strengthens the complicity of mankind, etc. . . .

I do not believe in desperate acts. I believe only in motivated acts. *But* I believe it takes very little to motivate an act.

There is no objection to the totalitarian attitude other than the religious or moral objection. If this world has no meaning, they are right. I do not accept that they are right. Hence . . .

It is up to us to create God. He is not the creator. That is the whole history of Christianity. For we have but one way of creating God, which is to become him.

Novel on Justice.

At the end. In the presence of the poor, sick mother.

"I'm not worried about you, Jean. You are intelligent."

"No, Mother, that's not it. I have often made mistakes

and I haven't always been a just man. But there is one thing . . ."

"Of course."

"There is one thing, and that is that I have never betrayed you. All my life I have been faithful to you."

"You are a good son, Jean. I know that you are a very good son."

"Thank you, Mother."

"No, it's for me to thank you rather. And for you to continue as you are."

There is no freedom for man so long as he has not overcome his fear of death. But not through suicide. In order to overcome, one must not surrender. Be able to die courageously without bitterness.

Heroism and saintliness, secondary virtues. But one must have stood the test.

Novel on Justice. A rebel who performs an act knowing that it will cause the death of innocent hostages . . . Then he agrees to sign the pardon of a writer he despises.

Reputation. It is given you by second-rate people and you share it with second-rate people or rascals.

Grace?

We must serve justice because our condition is unjust, increase happiness and joy because this universe is unhappy. Likewise, we must not condemn others to death because we have been given the death sentence.

The doctor, an enemy of God: he fights against death.

Plague. Rieux said he was the enemy of God because he was fighting against death and that it was even his function to be the enemy of God. He also said that by trying to save Paneloux he was proving to him at the same time that he was wrong and that by accepting being saved Paneloux was accepting the possibility of not being right. Paneloux told him merely that he would end up being right since beyond a doubt he himself would die, and Rieux replied that the essential was not to give in and to fight to the bitter end.

Meaning of my work: So many men are deprived of grace. How can one live without grace? One has to try it and do what Christianity never did: be concerned with the damned.

Classicism is domination of passions. Passions were individual in the classic age. Today they are collective. Collective passions must be dominated; in other words, given a form. But at the same time you experience them you are consumed by them. This is why most works of our period are reportages and not works of art.

Reply: if you can't do everything at once, give up everything. What does that mean? It requires more strength and will than were necessary. We shall succeed. The great classic of the future is an unequalled conqueror.

Novel on Justice. The fellow who rallies revolutionaries (Comm.). After judgment or suspicion (because unity is essential), he is at once given a mission in which everyone knows that death is inevitable. He accepts because this is in the order of things. He dies on the mission.

Id. The fellow who applies the ethics of sincerity to assert solidarity. His vast final solitude.

Id. We kill the toughest among them. They have killed the toughest of us. This leaves the functionaries and the jackasses. That's what it is to have ideas.

Plague. A chapter on fatigue.

Revolt. Liberty is the right not to lie. True on the social plane (subaltern and superior) and on the moral plane.

Creation corrected.[6] Story of the appointed suicide.

Plague. "The things that moan at being separated."

He (a railway inspector) lives solely for railways.
The railway employee lives on the thin surface of matter.

M.V.'s cousin. He collects montgolfier balloons (of china, made into tobacco pipes, paperweights, inkwells, etc.).

[6] This title reappears frequently in the *Notebooks,* and especially in Notebook V—"Creation corrected, or The System."

Universal novel. The tank that turns over and falls apart like a centipede.

Bob attacking in the summer meadows. His helmet covered with wallflowers and wild grasses.

Creation corrected

The tank that turns over and struggles like a centipede.

Bob in the summer meadows of Normandy. His helmet covered with wild grasses and wallflowers.

See report of the English commission on atrocities in *The Times.*

Suzy's Spanish journalist (ask for his text)—children point out corpses to him as they laugh.

Profound spiritual dejection for an hour.

All day long they talk of having a milk soup at supper because it makes one piss several times during the night. That the toilet is a hundred yards from the dormitory, that it's cold, etc.

Deported women as they come into Switzerland burst out laughing on seeing a funeral: "So that's the way they treat the dead here."

Jacqueline.

The two Polish boys of fourteen whose house is burned down with their parents in it. From fourteen to seventeen, Buchenwald.

The concierge for the Gestapo occupying two floors of an apartment house in rue de la Pompe. In the morning, she does the cleaning surrounded by people who have been tortured. "I never pay attention to what my tenants are doing."

Jacqueline on her way back from Koenigsberg to Ravensbruck—sixty miles on foot. In a large tent divided into four by a canvas stretcher. So many women that they can't sleep on the ground without fitting together like pieces of a puzzle. Dysentery. The toilet a hundred yards away. But one must climb over and step on bodies. They do it right there.

Universal aspect in the dialogue of politics and ethics. Opposite that conglomeration of gigantic forces: Sintès.[7]

X. a deported woman, liberated with a tattoo on her skin: Served for a year in the SS camp of . . .

Demonstration. That abstraction is evil. It causes wars, tortures, violence, etc. Problem: How does the abstract view continue in the face of physical evil, ideology in the face of the torture inflicted in the name of that ideology?

Christianity. You would certainly be punished if we accepted your postulates. For then your condemnation would be merciless.

Sade. Autopsy by Gall: "The bare skull resembled all the skulls of old men. The organs of paternal affection and the love of children are prominent."

Sade on Mme de La Fayette: "And as she became more concise, she became more interesting."

Sade's passionate admiration for Rousseau and Richardson, from whom he learned that "it's not always by making virtue win out that one interests."

Id. "One acquires knowledge of man's heart" only through misfortunes and travels.

[7] The few letters preceding *Sintès* are illegible.

Id. The man of the eighteenth century: "When, like the Titans, he dares to raise his bold hand against heaven and, armed with his passions, no longer fears declaring war on those who struck fear in him."

Revolt. Eventually politics leads to the parties that contribute to communication (complicity).[8]

And creation itself. What to do about it? It's the rebel who has *the least chance* of avoiding accomplices. But they will be so.

Utter disgust for all society. Temptation to flee and to accept the decadence of one's era. Solitude makes me happy. But feeling too that decadence begins the moment one accepts. And one stays—so that man will stay on the heights that belong to him. Exactly, so as not to contribute to his descent. But disgust, nauseating disgust for such dispersion in others.

Communication. A hindrance for man because he cannot go beyond the circle of people he knows. Beyond, he makes an abstraction of them. Man *must live* in the circle of flesh.

The aging heart. To have loved and yet that nothing can be saved.

---

[8] In the manuscript the word *complicité* is written over the word *communication.*

The temptation of menial and daily tasks.

C. and P.G.: the passion for truth. Around them, everyone is crucified.

We French are now in the van of all civilization: we
no longer know how to put to death.
We are the ones who bear witness against God.

JULY '45

Chateaubriand to Ampère going to Greece in 1841:
"Make my farewell to Mount Hymettus, where I left bees,
to Cape Sounion, where I heard crickets . . . I shall soon
have to forsake everything. I still wander in my memory
amid my recollections; but they will fade away . . . You will
not find a single olive leaf or a grape that I saw in Attica.
I regret even the grass of my time. I didn't have the strength
to keep a heather alive."

Revolt.
Finally, I choose liberty. For even if justice is not
realized, liberty maintains the power of protest against injustice and keeps communication open. Justice in a silent
world, the justice of mute men, destroys complicity, negates
revolt, and restores consent, but in the lowest possible
form. That's where one sees the priority gradually go to
the value of liberty. But the difficult thing is never to lose
sight of the fact that liberty must *at the same time* insist
upon justice, as has been said. Once this is established,
there is a justice likewise, though quite different, in laying

the foundation of the only constant value in the history of men, who have never really died except for liberty.

Liberty is the ability to defend what I do not think, even in a regime or a world that I approve. It is the ability to admit that the adversary is right.

"The man who repents is tremendous. But who today would like to be tremendous without being seen?" (*Life of Rancé*)[9]

The man I should be if I had not been the child I was.

Unpublished writings of Ch.

"I have never been hugged by a woman with that utter surrender, those double knots, that ardent passion I have sought and whose charm would be worth a lifetime."

"There are times when character being devoid of energy, vices produce only corruption instead of crimes."

Id. "If there were no passion, there would be no virtue, and yet this century has reached such a depth of wretchedness that it is without passion and without virtue; it does good and evil, while remaining passive like matter."

"When one has a noble mind and a mean heart, one writes great things and does only small ones."

Novel

"I gave men their share. In other words, I lied and desired with them. I rushed from person to person; I did what

9 Chateaubriand's *Vie de Rancé* (1844) tells the story of the seventeenth-century founder of the monastic order of Trappists.

was necessary. Now, that's enough. I have an account to settle with this landscape. I want to be alone with it."

JULY 30, 1945

At the age of thirty, a man ought to have control over himself, know the exact reckoning of his faults and virtues, recognize his limit, foresee his weakness—be what he is. And above all accept them. We are entering a positive period. Everything to be done and everything to be forsaken. Settle in to being natural, but with a mask. I have known enough things to be able to surrender almost everything. There remains an amazing effort, daily, insistent. The effort of the hidden, without hope or bitterness. No longer negate anything since everything can be asserted. Better than heartbreak.

NOTEBOOK V

September 1945 – April 1948

The only contemporary problem: Can one transform the world without believing in the absolute power of reason? Despite rationalistic, even Marxist, illusions, the whole history of the world is the history of liberty. How could the paths of liberty be determined? It is doubtless false to say that what is determined is what has ceased to live. Yet nothing is determined but what has been lived. God himself, if he existed, could not modify the past. But the future belongs to him neither more nor less than to man.

Political antinomies. We are in a world in which we must choose between being a victim or an executioner—and nothing else. Such a choice is not easy. It always seemed to me that in fact there were no executioners—

only victims. In the last analysis, of course. But this is a truth that is not widely known.

I have a very keen liking for liberty. And for any intellectual, liberty is eventually confused with freedom of expression. But I am quite aware that this concern is not the primary one of a very large number of Europeans because justice alone can give them the material minimum they need and rightly or wrongly they would gladly sacrifice liberty to that elementary justice.

I have known that for a long time. If I found it necsesary to defend the reconciliation of justice and liberty it is because I thought the last hope of the West lay in such a reconciliation. But such a reconciliation can be brought about only in a certain climate which today almost strikes me as Utopian. One or the other of these values must be sacrificed? What to think, in that case?

Politics (continued). Everything derives from the fact that those who have the responsibility of speaking for the masses don't have, never have, a real concern for liberty. When they are sincere, they even boast of the contrary. But the mere concern would be enough . . .

Consequently those—and they are few—who live with this scruple must perish some day or other (there are several ways of dying in this regard). If they are proud, they will not do so without having put up a fight. But how could they fight properly against their brothers and all justice? They will bear witness, that's all. And after two millennia we shall see the sacrifice, several times repeated, of Socrates. Program for tomorrow: solemn and significant execution of the witnesses of liberty.

Revolt: Create in order to return to mankind? But little by little creation separates us from everyone and sets us apart without the shadow of a love.

People always think that a man commits suicide for a reason. But he may very well commit suicide for *two* reasons.

We are not born for liberty. But determinism likewise is a mistake.

What could be (What is)[1] immortality for me? Living until the last man has disappeared from the earth. Nothing more.

X. This odd character talks and says nothing. But she is the opposite of frivolous. She speaks, and then contradicts herself or admits without discussion that she is wrong. All this because she considers it unimportant. She doesn't really think of what she is saying, concerned as she is with another wound, infinitely more serious, that she will drag about with her, unknown, unto death.

Aesthetics of revolt.[2] If classicism is defined by the domination of passions, a classical era is one whose art shapes and codifies the passions of the contemporaries. Today when collective passions have won out over indi-

---

[1] The words *Qu'est-ce que* were penciled on the manuscript.

[2] See preface to Chamfort's *Maximes et anecdotes* and the last chapter of *The Rebel*.

vidual passions, it is no longer a matter of dominating love through art, but of dominating politics, in the purest sense. Man has developed a passion, hopeful or destructive, for his condition.

But how much more difficult the task is (1) because, if passions must be experienced before being formulated, the collective passion consumes all the artist's time; (2) because the chances of death are greater, and indeed the only way of living the collective passion authentically is to be willing to die for it. In this case then, the greatest chance of authenticity is also the greatest chance of failure for art. Wherefor this classicism is perhaps impossible. But if it were, it is so because truly the history of human revolt has a meaning, which was to lead to this limit. Hegel would be right and the end of history would be imaginable, but only in a failure. And here Hegel would be wrong. But if, as we seem to believe, this classicism is possible, at least we see that it can be built up only by a generation— and not by an individual. In other words, the chances of failure I mention can be offset only by the chance of numbers—that is, the chance that out of ten authentic artists one will survive and manage to find in his life time for passion and time for creation. The artist can no longer be a solitary. Or, if he is, then he owes his triumph to a whole generation.

OCTOBER '45
AESTHETICS OF REVOLT

Impossibility for man to despair utterly. Conclusion: any literature of despair represents but an extreme case and not the most significant. The remarkable thing in man is not that he despairs, but that he overcomes or forgets despair. A literature of despair will never be universal.

Universal literature cannot stop at despair (nor at optimism either; just reverse the reasoning); it must merely take despair into account. To be added: reasons for which literature is or is not universal.

Aesthetics of revolt. High style and beautiful form, expressions of the loftiest revolt.

Creation corrected
"Men like me are not afraid of death," he said. "It's an accident that proves them right."

Why am I an artist and not a philosopher? Because I think according to words and not according to ideas.

Aesthetics of revolt
E. Forster[3]— "[The work of art] is the only material object in the universe which may possess internal harmony. All the others have been pressed into shape from outside, and when their mould is removed they collapse. The work of art stands up by itself, and nothing else does. *It achieves something which has often been promised by society, but always delusively.*"

". . . It (art) is the one orderly product which our muddling race has produced. It is the cry of a thousand sentinels, the echo from a thousand labyrinths; it is the lighthouse which cannot be hidden: *c'est le meilleur*

3 Both quotations are from "Art for Art's Sake," an address delivered in New York in 1949, and published in *Two Cheers for Democracy*, by E. M. Forster (Harcourt, Brace, 1951), p. 92. The italics in the first are Camus's; the French in the second is Forster's.

*témoignage que nous puissions donner de notre dig-
nité.*"

Id. Shelley: "Poets are the unacknowledged legislators of
the world."

Tragedy

C. and L. — "I come to you in this emergency. I am sending you into mortal danger."

"All of them are right," a character shouts.

C. — "I am sending you to an almost certain death. But
I insist that you understand me."

"I cannot understand what is inhuman."

"So I shall have to give up also being understood by
those I love."

C. — "I do not believe in liberty. That is my human
suffering. Today's liberty embarrasses me."

L. — "Why?"

"It keeps me from establishing justice."

"My conviction is that they can be reconciled."

"History shows that your conviction is wrong. I believe
they are not reconciled. That is my human wisdom."

"Why choose this rather than that?"

"Because I want the largest possible number of men to
be happy. And because liberty is never the concern, the
primary concern, of any but a few."

"And if you have missed your justice?"

"Then I shall enter a hell that even today you cannot
imagine."

"I'm going to tell you what will happen" (tableau).

"Each man bets on what he believes to be the truth . . ."

"Let me repeat, liberty embarrasses me— We must suppress the witnesses of liberty."

C. — "L., your esteem?"

L. — "What does that matter to you?"

C. — "You are right; it's a weakness that has no meaning."

L. — "Yet it is that weakness that makes me maintain my esteem for you. Farewell, C. . . . Men like me always look as if they were dying alone. That is what I am going to do. But in truth I shall have done the necessary to keep men from being alone."

L. — "Remaking the world is an insignificant task."

C. — "It is not the world that must be remade, but man."

C. — "There are fools everywhere. But everywhere else there are fools and cowards. Among us, you won't find a single coward."

L. — "Heroism is a secondary virtue."

C. — "*You* have a right to say so because you are showing your mettle. But what will be the primary virtue then?"

L. — (looking at him) — "Friendship."

L. — "If the world is tragic, if we live torn asunder, it is not so much because of tyrants. You and I know that there is a liberty, a justice, a deep, shared joy, a common fight against the tyrants. When evil dominates, there is no problem. When the adversary is wrong, those who are fighting him are free and at peace. But the split develops because men equally eager for the good of mankind either want it at once or else aim for three generations from now, and that is enough to divide them forever. When the adversaries are both right, then we enter tragedy. And at the end of tragedy, you know what there is?"

C. — "Yes, there is death."

L. — "Yes, there is death. And yet I shall never agree to kill you."

C. — "I should consent if it were necessary. That is my ethic. And it's the sign for me that you are not in the path of truth."

L. — "It's the sign for me that you are not in the path of truth."

C. — "I seem to be winning out because I am alive. But I am in the same night as you, having no other help than my human will."

End. L.'s body is brought back. A partisan treats it frivolously. Silence. C.: "This man died as a hero for the cause that was ours. It is up to us to respect him and to avenge him."[4]

C. — "Look. Look at this night. It is vast. It revolves its mute stars above frightful human battles. Through millennia you have adored this sky though it was obstinately silent, you accepted the fact that your paltry loves, your desires, and your fears were nothing compared with the divinity. You believed in your solitude. And today when you are asked to make the same sacrifice, but to serve humanity this time, will you refuse?"

C. — "Do not take me for an utterly blind soul."

L. returns wounded.

C. — "You should have got through anyway."

[4] The manuscript is almost illegible at this point.

L. — "It wasn't possible."
C. — "Since you were able to come back, you could have got through."
L. — "It wasn't possible."
C. — "Why?"
L. — "Because I am going to die."

X. — "It's not up to you to go."
C. — "I'm the leader here, and I'm the one to decide."
X. — "It so happens that we need you. We are not here to perform noble deeds, but to be efficient. A good leader is the condition of efficiency."
C. — "You're right, X. But I don't much like truths that turn to my advantage. Hence I'll go."

The F. — "But who is right then?"
The lieutenant — "The one who survives."
A man comes in: "He too died."[5]
Oh! no, no! And *I* know for sure who was right. It was he, yes, he who called for a reconciliation.

Revolt.
Collective passions win out over individual passions. Men no longer know how to love. What interests them today is the human condition and not individual fates.

Liberty is the last of individual passions. That's why it is immoral today. Both in society, and in itself, to be sure, liberty is immoral.

Philosophy is the contemporary form of indecency.

[5] These three lines were penciled on the manuscript.

At the age of thirty, almost overnight, I knew fame. I don't regret it. I might have had nightmares about it later on. Now I know what it is. It's not much.

Thirty articles.[6] The reason for the praise is as bad as the reason for the criticism. Scarcely one or two authentic voices or voices moved to emotion. Fame! In the best of cases, a misunderstanding. But I shall not assume the superior look of someone who disdains fame. It too is a mark of men, neither more nor less important than their indifference, than friendship, than hatred. What does all that matter to me in the end? This misunderstanding, for anyone who knows how to take it, is a deliverance. My ambition, if I have one, is of a different nature.

N O V E M B E R — thirty-two years old

Man's most natural inclination is to ruin himself and everyone with him. What exceptional efforts he must make to be merely normal! And what an even greater effort for anyone who has an ambition to dominate himself and to dominate the mind. Man is nothing in himself. He is but an infinite chance. But he is infinitely responsible for that chance. By himself, man is inclined to water himself down. But the moment his will, his conscience, his spirit of adventure dominates, chance begins to increase. No one can say that he has reached the limit of man. The five years we have just lived through taught me that. From the animal to the martyr, from the spirit of evil to hopeless sacrifice, every testimony was staggering. Each of us has the responsibility of exploiting in himself man's greatest chance, his definitive virtue. When the human

6 After the production of *Caligula*.

limit finally has a meaning, then the problem of God will arise. But not before then, never before the possibility has been fully experienced. There is but one possible aim for great deeds and that is human productiveness. *But first of all make oneself master of oneself.*

Tragedy is not a solution.

Parain. God did not create himself. He is the son of human pride.
To understand is to create.

Revolt. If man fails in reconciling justice and liberty, then he fails in everything. And religion is right? No, if he accepts approximation.

It requires bucketsful of blood and centuries of history to lead to an imperceptible modification in the human condition. Such is the law. For years heads fall like hail, Terror reigns, Revolution is touted, and one ends up by substituting constitutional monarchy for legitimate monarchy.

I lived my whole youth with the idea of my innocence, in other words with no idea at all. Today . . .

I am not made for politics because I am incapable of wanting or accepting the death of the adversary.

Only by a continual effort can I create. My tendency is to drift toward immobility. My deepest, surest inclination lies in silence and the daily routine. To escape relaxation, the fascination of the mechanical, it took years of perseverance. But I know that I stand erect through that very effort and that if I ceased to believe in it for a single moment I should roll over the precipice. This is how I avoid illness and renunciation, raising my head with all my strength to breathe and to conquer. This is my way of despairing and this is my way of curing myself.

Our task: to create universality or at least universal values. Win for man his catholicity.

Historical materialism, absolute determinism, the negation of all liberty, that frightful world of courage and silence—these are the most legitimate consequences of a philosophy without God. This is where Parain is right. If God does not exist, nothing is permitted. Christianity alone is strong in this regard. For to the divinization of history it will always raise the objection of the creation of history; it will inquire of the existentialist situation whence its origin, etc. But its replies do not come from reasoning; they come from mythology that calls for faith.

What to do between the two? Something in me tells me, convinces me that I cannot detach myself from my era without cowardice, without accepting slavery, without denying my mother and my truth. I could not do so, or accept a commitment that was both sincere and relative, unless I were a Christian. Not a Christian, I must go on to the end. But going on to the end means choosing history absolutely, and with it the murder of man if the murder of man is necessary to history. Otherwise, I am but a witness. That is the question: can I be merely a witness? In other words: have I the right to be merely an artist? I cannot believe so. If I do not choose both against God and against history, I am the witness of pure liberty whose fate in history is to be put to death.[7] In the present state of things, my situation lies in silence or death. If I choose to do violence to myself and to believe in history, my situation will be falsehood and murder. Outside that, religion. I understand that a man can hurl himself into religion blindly to escape this madness and this painful (yes, really painful) laceration. But I cannot do it.

. Consequence: Have I the right, as an artist still attached to liberty, to accept the advantages in money and consideration that are linked to that attitude? The reply for me would be simple. It is in poverty that I have found and shall always find the conditions essential to keep my culpability, if it exists, from being shameful at least and to keep it proud. But must I reduce my children to poverty, refuse even the very modest comfort I am preparing for them? And in these conditions, was I wrong to accept the simplest human tasks and duties, such as having children? In the end, has one the right to have children, to assume the human condition[8] when one doesn't believe in God (add the intermediary arguments)?

How easy it would be if I yielded to the horror and disgust that this world gives me, if I could still believe that man's task is to create happiness! Keep silent at least, keep silent, keep silent, until I feel I have the right . . .

[7] Or to cheat by enjoying the material advantages of the privileged artist. [*Author's note.*]

[8] Moreover, did I really assume it when I felt such hesitation and still have trouble doing so? Does not this inconstant heart deserve such a contradiction? [*Author's note.*]

Creation corrected.

Under the Occupation: the gatherers of dung. The suburban gardens.

Saint-Étienne Dunières: The workmen in the same compartment as German soldiers. A bayonet has disappeared. The soldiers hold the workmen until Saint-Étienne. The big fellow who was to get off at Firminy. His rage on the verge of tears. Added to the face's fatigue, the even more cruel fatigue of humiliation.

We are asked to choose between God and history. Whence this dreadful longing to choose the earth, the world, and trees, if I were not absolutely sure that all mankind does not coincide with history.

All philosophy is a justification of oneself. The only original philosophy would be the one that would justify someone else.

Against the literature of commitment. Man is not *only* social. His death at least belongs to him. We are made to live in relation to others. But one dies truly only for oneself.

Aesthetics of revolt. Thibaudet[9] of Balzac: *"The Human Comedy* is the imitation of God the Father." The theme of revolt, of the outlaw, in Balzac.

[9] Albert Thibaudet (1874–1936) was a vigorous and always original critic of French literature.

80% of divorces among repatriated prisoners. 80% of human loves do not resist five years of separation.

Thomas: "Eh . . . what was I saying? Well, it'll come back to me in a moment . . . In any case, Roupp said to me: 'You see, I'm the manager of a boxer. I'd like to manage a painter too. So, if you wish . . .' I didn't wish; I like my freedom. And then, Roupp suggested I set out for Paris. Of course, I accepted. I eat at his house. He got me a room in a hotel. He's paying it all. He is pushing me now to work."

X. — A modest and charitable satanism.

A tragedy on the problem of evil. The best of men must be damned if he serves only man.

"We love people less for the good they have done us than for the good we have done them." No, in the worst of cases, we love them equally. And it's not a misfortune. It is natural that we should be grateful to someone who allows us at least once to be better than we are. It's a better conception of man that we revere and acknowledge in this way.

By what right would a Communist or a Christian (to take only the respectable forms of modern thought) blame me for being a pessimist? *I* didn't invent human misery or the terrible formulas of divine malediction. *I* didn't say that man was incapable of saving himself alone and that from the depths in which he wallows he had no definitive hope save in the grace of God. As for the famous Marxist optimism, allow me to laugh. Few men have carried further distrust of their fellow men. Marxists do not believe in persuasion or in dialogue. A workman cannot be made out of a bourgeois, and economic conditions are in their world more terrible fatalities than divine whims.

As for M. Herriot and the subscribers to *Les Annales!*[1]

Communists and Christians will tell me that their optimism looks further ahead, that it is superior to all the rest, and that God or history, according to the case, is the satisfactory aim of their dialectic. I have the same reasoning to make. If Christianity is pessimistic as to man, it is optimistic as to human destiny. Marxism, pessimistic as to destiny, pessimistic as to human nature, is optimistic as to the progress of history (its contradiction!). *I* shall say that, pessimistic as to the human condition, I am optimistic as to mankind.

How can they fail to see that never has such confidence in man been expressed? I believe in the dialogue, in sincerity. I believe they are the means to an unequaled psychological revolution; etc., etc. . . .

Hegel: "Only the modern city offers the mind the terrain in which it can be conscious of itself." Significant. This is the time of big cities. The world has been amputated of a part of its truth, of what makes its permanence and its equilibrium: nature, the sea, etc. There is consciousness only in city streets!

(Cf. Sartre, all the modern philosophies of history, etc.)

[1] Édouard Herriot (1872–1957), several times premier of France, sponsored the conservative and popular periodical of this name.

Revolt. The human effort toward liberty and its *habitual* contradiction: discipline and liberty die at their own hands. Revolution must accept its own violence or be denied. Consequently it cannot take place in purity, but only in blood and selfish motives. My effort: show that the logic of revolt rejects blood and selfish motives. And that the dialogue carried to the absurd gives *a* chance to purity. — Through compassion? (suffer together)

Plague. "Let's not exaggerate anything," Tarrou said. "The plague exists. We must defend ourselves against it and that's what we are doing. Truly it's a small matter and in any case it doesn't prove anything."

The airfield is too far from town to set up a regular service. They simply send packages by parachute.

After Tarrou's death, the telegram is received announcing Mme Rieux's death.

The plague follows the course of the year. It has its springtime when it germinates and flowers, its summer and its autumn, etc. . . .

To Guilloux:[2] "The whole misfortune of men comes from the fact that they don't use a simple speech. If the hero of *The Misunderstanding* had said: 'Well, here I am and I am your son,' the dialogue would have been possible and not at cross-purposes as in the play. There would have been no tragedy because the height of all tragedies lies in the deafness of the protagonists. From this point of view, Socrates is the one who is right, against Jesus and Nietzsche. Progress and true nobility lie in the dialogue from man

[2] A socialist imbued with a deep love of humanity, Louis Guilloux (1899–) wrote novels dealing with the working class. Camus wrote the preface for the reprint of one of these, *La Maison du peuple*, in 1953.

to man and not in the Gospel, a monologue and dictated from the top of a solitary mountain. That's where I stand. What balances the absurd is the community of men fighting against it. And if we choose to serve that community, we choose to serve the dialogue carried to the absurd against any policy of falsehood or of silence. That's the way one is free with others."

The limits. Thus I shall say that there are mysteries it is suitable to enumerate and to meditate. Nothing more.

Saint-Just: "I think then that we must be impassioned. This does not exclude common sense or wisdom."

For a thought to change the world, it must first change the life of the man who carries it. It must become an example.

At the age of twelve she is raped by a coachman. Just once. Until the age of seventeen, she has the idea of a sort of defilement.

Creation corrected. The two Jews of Verdelot during the Occupation. The dreadful obsession of arrest. She becomes mad and goes and denounces him. Then she comes and warns him. They are found hanged together. The bitch howling all night long, as in the most ordinary of thrillers.

Creation corrected: "I had always been told that you had to seize immediately the first opportunity to escape. Any risk was better than what would follow. But it is easier to remain a prisoner and to let yourself drift toward the horror than to escape. Because in the latter case you have to take the initiative. In the first, others take it."

Id. "If you really want to know, I never believed in the Gestapo. Because you never saw it. To be sure, I took my precautions, but abstractly in a way. From time to time, a pal would disappear. Another day, in front of Saint-Germain-des-Prés, I saw two big fellows pushing a man into a taxi while pummeling his face. And no one said anything. A café waiter said to me: 'Keep quiet. It's them.' That gave me a hint that they really existed and that some day . . . But only a hint. The truth is that I could never believe in the Gestapo until I got kicked in the belly myself. That's the way I am. And that's why you mustn't have too exalted an idea of my courage because I am in the Resistance, as they say. No, it's no credit to me because I have no imagination."

Politics of revolt. "Thus it is that the pessimistic revolution becomes the revolution of happiness."

Tragedy. C.L.C. "I am right and that's what gives me the right to kill him. I can't hesitate over that detail. I think according to the world and history."
L. — "When the detail is a human life, for me it is the whole world and all of history."

Origins of the modern madness. It was Christianity that turned man away from the *world*. It reduced him to himself and to his history. Communism is a logical successor to Christianity. It is a history of Christians.

Id. After two thousand years of Christianity, the body's revolt. Two thousand years before we could again exhibit it naked on beaches. Whence excess. And the body found its place in usage. It remains to give it that place again in philosophy and metaphysics. This is one of the meanings of the modern convulsion.

Fair criticism of the absurd by Albert Wild: "The *feeling* of anguish is irreconcilable with the *feeling* of liberty."

The Greeks made allowance for the divine. But *the divine was not everything.*

"But let your communication be, Yea, yea; Nay, nay: for whatsoever is more than these cometh of evil." Matt. 5:37.

Koestler. The extreme doctrine: "Whoever is opposed to dictatorship must accept civil war as a means. Whoever baulks at civil war must give up the opposition and accept the dictatorship." That is the typical "historical" reasoning.

Id. "It (the Party) denied the free will of the individual —and at the same time demanded of him a voluntary abnegation. It denied that he had the possibility of choosing between two solutions and at the same time it demanded that he constantly choose the right one. It denied that he had the faculty of distinguishing between good and evil—and at the same time it spoke emotionally of guilt and treachery. The individual—a cog in a clockwork which was wound up for eternity and which nothing could stop or influence—was dominated by economic fatality and the Party demanded that the cog should revolt against the clockwork and change its motion."

Typical of the "historical" contradiction.

Id. "The greatest temptation for men like us is to renounce violence, to repent, to be at peace with oneself. God's temptations have always been more dangerous for humanity than those of Satan."

Novel of love: Jessica.

Death of an old actor.
One morning in a snowy, muddy Paris. The oldest and most melancholy section in town, the one that houses the Santé, Sainte-Anne, and Cochin.[3] Along the dark, icy streets, the insane, the sick, the poor, and the condemned. As for Cochin: the barracks of poverty and illness, and its walls drip with the filthy humidity that belongs to misfortune.

That is where he died. At the end of his life, he was still playing bit parts (utility men, as theater people call them), changing his single threadbare suit yellowing with

[3] On the Boulevard de Port-Royal, near the Métro station of La Glacière, are grouped the Cochin hospital and prisons like La Santé and Sainte-Anne.

age for the more or less glittering costumes that have to be provided, willy-nilly, for the minor roles. He had to give up his work. He could no longer drink anything but milk, and besides he had no milk. He was taken to Cochin and he told his friends that he was going to be operated on and then it would be all over. (I recall a line from his part: "When I was a little child," and as a suggestion was made to him about its delivery, "Ah!" he said, "I don't feel it that way.") He wasn't operated on but was sent away, being told he was cured. He even went back to the bit part of a ludicrous little man that he was playing at that time. But he had lost weight. It has always amazed me to what degree the loss of a certain amount of weight, a certain manner of having the cheekbones stand out and the gums shrink, is the obvious sign that it's all coming to an end. The one who is losing weight is the only one who never seems to "be aware." Or if he "is aware," it's only intermittently perhaps, and I, of course, have no way of knowing. All I can know is what I see and it so happened that I saw that Liesse was going to die.

He died indeed. He stopped working again. He went back to Cochin. They still didn't operate, but he died without that—one night without a fuss. And in the morning his wife came to see him as usual. No one informed her at the office because no one had been informed. Those in the neighboring beds informed his wife. "You know," they said, "it happened last night."

And this morning there he is, in the little morgue opening on to the rue de la Santé. Two or three of his old associates are there with the widow and the widow's daughter, who is not his daughter. When I arrived, the undertaker (why was he wearing a tricolor sash like a mayor?) told me he could still be seen. I didn't want to; I still had this filthy, clinging morning stuck in my throat.

But I went. You could see only his head; what served as a shroud was pulled up to his chin. He had lost more weight; I didn't think anyone in his condition could get still thinner. Yet he had done so, and one could see the thickness of his bones and realize that this strong, nobby head was made to carry a heavy weight of flesh. For lack of flesh, the teeth jutted out, frighteningly . . . But am I going to describe that? A dead body is a dead body, as everyone knows, and the dead must be left to bury the dead. What a pity, though, what a dreadful pity!

The men who were at his head, their hands on the edge of the coffin as if they were presenting him to the visitor, then got under way. Got under way is the word, for those awkward, stiff automata in their coarse clothing suddenly hurled themselves upon the shroud, the cover, and a screwdriver. In a second the top was down and two men were tightening the screws, weighing heavily on them with a brutal motion of the forearm. "Ah!" they seemed to say, "you won't get out now!" Those living men wanted it over with, that could be seen at once. He was carried out. We followed him. The widow and the daughter climbed into the hearse at the same time as the corpse. We piled into a car that followed. Not a flower, nothing but black everywhere.

We were going to the Thiais Cemetery. The widow thought it was far, but the office had forced it on her. We left town by the Porte d'Italie. Never had the sky seemed to me so low over the suburbs of Paris. Fragments of shanties, stakes, a black, spotty vegetation emerged from the piles of snow and mud. Two or three miles of this landscape and we reached the monumental gates of the most hideous cemetery in the world. A guard with a red face came out to stop the procession at the gate and demanded the ticket. "O.K.," he said, once he had it in his hands. For some ten minutes we navigated amid piles of mud and snow. Then we stopped behind another funeral. We were separated from the field of the dead by an embankment of snow. In the snow two crosses were planted askew; one was for Liesse, from what I saw, and the other for a little girl eleven years old. The funeral ahead of us was the little girl's. But the family was just getting back into the hearse. It started off and we were able to advance a few yards. We got out. Tall fellows in blue wearing boots like sewermen dropped the shovels they were holding as they watched the scene. They stepped forward and began to pull the coffin out of the hearse. At that moment, a sort of mailman dressed in blue and red, wearing a bashed-in military cap, suddenly appeared with an invoice with carbon paper between the sheets. Then the sewermen read aloud a number engraved on the coffin: 3237 C. The mailman followed the lines of his invoice with his pencil and he said "O. K." as he checked a number. At that moment they pulled out the coffin. We entered the field. Our feet sank into an oily and elastic mud. The hole was dug among four other holes that surrounded it on all sides. The sewermen slipped the box in rather swiftly. But we were all very far from the hole because the graves kept us from stepping forward and the narrow passage separating them was cluttered with tools and with earth. When the coffin reached the bottom, there was a moment of silence. Everyone looked at one another. There was no priest, no flowers, and not a word of peace or of regret rose from the group. And all felt that the moment should be more solemn, that it should have been emphasized, and no one knew how. Then a sewerman said: "If these ladies and gentlemen want to throw in a little earth." The widow nodded yes. He picked up some earth on a shovel, took a trowel out of his pocket, and picked up some soil on the trowel. The widow stretched out her hand above a mound of earth. She took the trowel and threw the soil in the direction of the hole, rather wildly. The hollow sound of the box could be heard. But the daughter missed her shot. The soil went far beyond the hole. She made a gesture that meant: "Too bad."

The bill: "And he was put into the clay soil for an exorbitant price."

You know, this is the cemetery of the people put to death.

Laval is a little farther on.

[*The trip to North America (March–May 1946) comes at this point.*]

Novel. When supper was late, it was because there was to be an execution in the morning.

V. Ocampo[4] goes to Buckingham Palace. At the entrance the guard asks her where she is going. "To see the Queen." "Carry on." The flunky inside likewise. "Carry on." The Queen's apartments. "Take the lift." Etc. She is received without any other kind of interrogation.

Nuremberg. 60,000 bodies under the ruins. It is prohibited to drink the water. But one doesn't feel like washing in it either. It's water from the Morgue. Above the decomposition, the trial.

On the lampshades made of human skin can be seen a very ancient dancer tattooed between the nipples.

Revolt. Beginning: "The only really serious moral problem is murder. The rest comes after. But to find out whether or not I can kill this person in my presence, or agree to his being killed, to find that I know nothing before finding out whether or not I can cause death, that is what must be learned."

People always want to push us in the direction of *their* consequences. If they judge us, they always do so with their principles in mind. But *I* don't care what they think. What

---

[4] Victoria Ocampo, the Argentine writer who founded and edited the influential review *Sur* in Buenos Aires.

matters to me is to find out whether or not I can kill. Because you have reached the frontiers where all thought stumbles, they begin rubbing their hands. "And now, what is he going to do?" And they have their truth all ready. But I think I don't care if I am in a state of contradiction; I don't want to be a philosophical genius. I don't even want to be a genius at all, for I have enough trouble just being a man. I want to find an agreement, and, knowing that I cannot kill myself, to find out whether I can kill or let others be killed and, knowing it, to draw all the conclusions from it even if that is to leave me in a state of contradiction.

It seems that I still have to find a humanism. I have nothing against humanism, of course. I just find it inadequate. And Greek thought, for example, was quite different from a humanism. It was a thought that had room for everything.

The Terror! And they are already forgetting.

Novel on Justice.[5]
1) Poor childhood—injustice is natural.
    At the first example of violence (brutal interrogation, injustice, and adolescence in revolt).
2) Native politics. Party (etc.).
    Loves
3) Revolution in general. Does not think of principles. War and Resistance.
4) The purging of the collaborators. Justice cannot be reconciled with violence.

5 Passage reinstated by the French publishers.

5) That truth cannot be achieved without a true life.

6) Return to the mother. Priest? "It's not worthwhile." She didn't say "no." But that it wasn't worthwhile. He knew that she never thought it worthwhile to disturb someone for her. And even her death . . .

Revolt and Revolution.

The revolution as myth is the definitive revolution.

Id. Historicity leaves unexplained the phenomenon of beauty; in other words, relations with the world (sentiment of nature) and with persons as individuals (love). What to think of a supposedly absolute explanation that . . .

Id. The whole effort of German thought has been to substitute for the notion of human nature that of human situation and hence to substitute history for God and modern tragedy for ancient equilibrium. Modern existentialism carries that effort even further and introduces into the idea of situation the same uncertainty as in the idea of nature. Nothing remains but a motion. But like the Greeks I believe in nature.

Plague. In my whole life, never such a feeling of failure. I am not even sure of reaching the end. At certain moments, however . . .

Blow up everything. Give to revolt the form of a tract. Revolution and those who will never kill. Rebellious preaching. Not a single concession.

"What a mad, inconceivable thing that a writer cannot —in any conceivable circumstance—be frank with his readers." Melville.

From the point of view of a new classicism, *The Plague* ought to be the first attempt at shaping a collective passion.

For *The Plague.* See Defoe's preface to the third volume of *Robinson Crusoe* (*Serious Reflections during the Life and Surprising Adventures of Robinson Crusoe*): ". . . It is as reasonable to represent one kind of imprisonment by another, as it is to represent anything that really exists by that which exists not. . . . Had the common way of writing a man's private history been taken . . . all I could have said would have yielded no diversion . . ."[6]

The Plague is a *tract.*

How can one learn how to die in the desert!

Lourmarin.[7] First evening, after so many years. The first star above the Lubéron, the vast silence, the cypress with its tip shivering in the depths of my fatigue. Solemn and austere landscape—despite its bewildering beauty.

[6] Camus used the first sentence of this quotation from Defoe as an epigraph to *La Peste* in 1947, and many assumed that it came from *A Journal of the Plague Year.*

[7] Invited by Henri Bosco, Camus went to Lourmarin with several other writers. In late 1958 he bought a house in that small village in the Durance Valley about twenty-five miles from Aix-en-Provence, and two years later he was buried in the local cemetery, which is within sight of the small mountain known as Le Lubéron.

Story of the former deportee who encounters German prisoners in Lourmarin. "The first time he had been struck was during his interrogation. Normal enough in a way considering the exceptional circumstance. But in the camp, when he received two hard slaps for some little mistake in his service, it all began. For then he realized that in the eyes of the man who had struck him it was normal, natural, customary . . ." He tries to talk to the German prisoner to explain what he means. But the other is a *prisoner;* one can't talk to him about that. Eventually the fellow disappears, without his having talked to him. On second thought, he feels that no man is ever free enough to be able to throw light on that. They are all prisoners.

Another time, in the camp, the Germans had amused themselves by making them dig their own graves and then had not executed them. For two full hours they had dug in the black earth, seen the roots, etc., with new eyes.

"It's dying without death and accomplishing nothing
To waver thus
In the dark belly of cramped misfortune."
                                        Agrippa d'Aubigné

Revolt. First chapter on the death penalty.
Id. end. Thus, starting from the absurd, it is not possible to live revolt without reaching at some point or other an experience of love that is still undefined.

Novel. Poor childhood. "I was ashamed of my poverty and of my family. (But they are monsters!) And if I can speak of it today quite simply this is because I am no

longer ashamed of that shame and no longer despise myself for having felt it. I came to know such shame only
when I was sent to the *lycée*. Before then, everyone was
poor like me, and poverty seemed to me the very air
we breathed in this world. At school I came to know the
comparison.

"A child is nothing in himself. His parents represent
him. And one deserves much less credit, having reached
maturity, for not knowing such ugly feelings. For then
you are judged for what you are and you even go so far
as to judge your family by what you have become. I now
know it would have required a heart of heroic and exceptional purity not to suffer from those days when I used to
read on the face of a more favored friend the surprise he
couldn't hide on seeing the house where I lived.

"Yes, I lacked courage, and that is vulgar. And if until
the age of twenty-five I felt rage and shame at the memory
of that lack of courage, this is because I refused to be
vulgar. Whereas I know now that I am and, having ceased
to consider it either good or bad, I am interested in other
things . . .

"I loved my mother with despair. I have always loved
her with despair."

Idea of resistance in the metaphysical sense.

Treat of the harm the world does me. It makes me disparaging, whereas I am not . . . That sort of second
state . . .

Machado. "The sound of the coffin in the earth is an
utterly serious thing."

"O Lord, we are alone, my mother and my heart."
"When comes the day of my last voyage

And the ship sails that never returns,
You will find me on board with slim baggage
And almost naked like the sons of the sea."

Translate the speeches of Juan de Mairena.[8]
An African *romancero*?

The only great Christian mind that *faced* the problem
of evil was St. Augustine. He drew from it the terrible
"Nemo Bonus." Since then Christianity has striven to give
the problem temporary solutions.

The result is evident. For it is the result. Men took their
time, but today they are poisoned by an intoxication that
has been going on for two thousand years. They are fed
up with evil or resigned, and this comes to the same thing.
At least they can no longer accept lies on the subject.

February 19, 1861. Law suppressing serfdom in Russia.
The first shot (fired by Karakozov) was the 4th of April
1866.

See *Whose Fault?* a novel by Herzen (1847).

And *id. On the Development of Revolutionary Ideas in
Russia.*[9]

I prefer committed men to literatures of commitment.
Courage in one's life and talent in one's works—this is

---

[8] The Spanish poet Antonio Machado (1875–1939), whom Camus
quotes in French, attributed his philosophical aphorisms in prose to one
Juan de Mairena, a creation of his own mind.

[9] Readings for *The Just Assassins* and *The Rebel*. One of the few
Russian liberals in the middle of the nineteenth century, Alexander
Herzen (1812–70) left Russia in 1847 but was bitterly disappointed by
the European revolutions of 1848.

not so bad. And moreover the writer is committed when he wishes to be. His merit lies in his impulse. But if this is to become a law, a function, or a terror, just where is the merit?

It seems that to write a poem about spring today would be to serve capitalism. I am not a poet, but I should delight in such a work without mental reservation, if it were beautiful. One serves mankind all together or not at all. And if man needs bread and justice, and if we must do the necessary to satisfy that need, he also needs pure beauty, which is the bread of his heart. The rest is not serious.

Yes, I should like to see them less committed in their works and a little more so in their daily life.

Existentialism kept Hegelianism's basic error, which consists in reducing man to history. But it did not keep the consequence, which is to refuse in fact any liberty to man.

OCTOBER 1946. Thirty-three years old in a month

My memory has been slipping for the last year. Inability to remember a story told me—to recall whole sections of the past, which nonetheless were alive. Until it improves (if it does improve), obviously I must note here more and more things, even personal ones—too bad. For in the end everything takes its place for me on the same rather foggy plane, and forgetfulness has also reached my heart. I have ceased to have any but brief emotions, devoid of the long echo that memory gives. The sensitivity of dogs is like that.

Plague . . . "And every time I have read a story about plague, from the bottom of a heart poisoned by its own rebellions and by the violences of others there rose a clear cry saying that there were nevertheless in men more things to admire than things to despise."

. . . "And that everyone carries the plague in him, because no one, no one in the world, is untouched by it.[1] And that one must watch oneself constantly not to be led in a moment of distraction to breathe in someone else's face and to infect him. What is natural is the microbe. The rest, health, integrity, purity if you wish, is an effect of the will and of a will that must never relax. The admirable man, who does not infect anyone, is the man who has the fewest possible moments of distraction.

"Yes, it's tiring to be a skunk. But it's even more tiring not to want to be a skunk. This is why everyone is tired since everyone is somewhat of a skunk. But this is also why a few know an extremity of fatigue that nothing will cure short of death."

Of course, what interests *me* is not so much being better as being accepted. And no one accepts anyone. Did she accept me? No, it's quite obvious.

The look of poor animals that people have in a doctor's waiting room.

Jacques Rigaut: "The example comes from above. God created man in his image. What a temptation for man to live up to that image."

"The solution, the reply, the clue, the truth, is the death sentence."

[1] See Tarrou in *The Plague,* next to last chapter of IV.

"Presumptuous man, what does he, who is nothing, have to fear?"

"The greater my disinterestedness, the more authentic my interest."

"Either one of two things. Not to speak out, not to keep silent. Suicide."

"So long as I have not overcome my inclination for sensual pleasure, I shall be sensitive to the attraction of suicide, I am well aware."

Conversations with Koestler. The end justifies the means only if the relative order of importance is reasonable— ex.: I can send Saint-Exupéry on a fatal mission to save a regiment. But I cannot deport millions of persons and suppress all liberty for an equivalent quantitative result and compute for three or four generations previously sacrificed.

Genius. There is no such thing.

When he is recognized as a talent, the creator's great suffering begins (I no longer have the courage to publish my books.).

There are moments when I don't believe I can endure the contradiction any longer. When the sky is cold and nothing supports us in nature . . . Ah! better to die perhaps.

Continuation of the preceding. My anguish at the idea of doing those articles for *Combat*.[2]

2 Probably "Ni victimes ni bourreaux," published in November 1946 and included in *Actuelles I*.

An essay on the feeling for nature—and sensual pleasure.

Art and revolt. Breton is right. I don't believe either in the break between the world and man. There are the moments of harmony with crude nature. But nature is never crude. But landscapes are fleeting and soon forgotten. This is why there are painters. And surrealist painting *in its movement* is the expression of that revolt of man against Creation. But its mistake lay in trying to preserve or imitate only the miraculous side of nature. The true rebellious artist does not deny miracles; he overcomes them rather.

Parain. That the essence of modern literature is recantation. The surrealists becoming Marxists. Rimbaud, devotion. Sartre, ethics. And that the great problem of the moment is the conflict. Human condition. Human nature.

But if there is a human nature, where does it come from?

Obvious that I ought to give up all creative activity so long as I don't know. What constituted the success of my books is what constitutes their falsehood for me. In fact, I am an average man with an exigency. The values I ought to defend and illustrate today are average values. This requires a talent so spare and unadorned that I doubt I have it.

The aim of revolt is the pacification of men. Any revolt reaches the ultimate and reverberates in the assertion of human limits—and of a community of all men, whoever they are, within those limits. Humility and genius.

October 29. Koestler, Sartre, Malraux, Sperber, and I. Between Piero della Francesca and Dubuffet.[3]

K. — Necessity of defining a minimum political code of ethics. Hence of getting rid first of a certain number of false scruples, which he calls "fallacies" in English: (a) that what you say may serve causes you yourself cannot serve. (b) Soul-searching. The order of injustices. "When the interviewer asked me, for example, if I hated Russia, something came to a stop there in me. And I made an effort. I said that I hated the Stalin regime as much as I hated the Hitler regime and for the same reasons. But something came undone at that point." "So many years of struggle. I lied for them . . . and now like that friend who beat his head against the walls of my room, saying as he turned his blood-spattered face toward me: 'There is no more hope, there is no more hope.'" Modes of action, etc.

M. — Momentary impossibility of reaching the proletariat. Is the proletariat the highest historical value?

C. — Utopia. A Utopia today will cost them less than a war. The opposite of Utopia is war. On the one hand. On the other: "Don't you believe that we are all responsible for the absence of values? And that if all of us who come from Nietzscheism, from nihilism, or from historical realism said in public that we were wrong and that there are moral values and that in the future we shall do the neces-

[3] Soon after this meeting at the home of André Malraux, Sartre and David Rousset founded the R.D.R., which became a subject of controversy in French intellectual life.

sary to establish[4] and illustrate them, don't you believe this would be the beginning of a hope?"

S. — "I cannot turn my moral values solely against the U.S.S.R. For it is true that the deporting of several million men is more serious than the lynching of a Negro. But the lynching of a Negro is the result of a situation that has been going on for a hundred years and more, and that represents in the end the suffering of just as many millions of Negroes over the years as there are millions of Cherkess deported."

K. — It must be said that as writers we are guilty of treason in the eyes of history if we do not denounce what deserves to be denounced. The conspiracy of silence is our condemnation in the eyes of those who come after us.

S. — Yes. Etc., etc.

And during all this time the impossibility of determining how much fear or truth enters into what each one says.

If one believes in moral value, one believes in all morality, even and including sexual morality. The reform is total.

Read Owen.

Write the story of a contemporary cured of his heartbreaks solely by long contemplation of a landscape.

Robert, a conscientious objector of Communist sympathies, in '33. Three years in prison. When he gets out, the Communists are for war and the pacifists are on the

4 The word in the manuscript might be read as *garder* ("to preserve").

side of Hitler. He can't understand anything in this world gone mad. He signs up with the Spanish republicans and *goes off to war*. He is killed on the Madrid front.

What is a famous man? It's a man whose given name doesn't matter. With all others, the given name has a very specific meaning.

Why does one drink? Because in drink everything assumes importance, everything takes its place on the highest plane. Conclusion: one drinks through impotence and through condemnation.

The universal order cannot be built from above, in other words through an idea; but rather from below, in other words through the common basis which . . .

Prepare a book of political texts around Brasillach.[5]

Guilloux. The only reference is pain. So that the guiltiest of men will maintain a relation with the human.

Met Tar. as I came away from the public statement I made concerning dialogue. He seems reticent, yet has the same friendly look in his eyes that he had when I recruited him into the Combat network.

[5] A brilliant disciple of Charles Maurras, Robert Brasillach (1910–45) was executed in February 1945 for collaboration with the Germans during the Occupation. There has been a vigorous campaign to rehabilitate him.

"You're a Marxist now?"

"Yes."

"Then you'll be a murderer."

"I've already been one."

"I too. But I don't want to be any more."

"You were my sponsor."

That was true.

"Listen, Tar. This is the real problem: whatever happens, I shall always defend you against the firing squad. But you will be obliged to approve my being shot. Think about that."

"I'll think about it."

Unbearable solitude—I cannot believe it or resign myself to it.

What makes a man feel alone is the cowardice of others. Must one try to understand that cowardice too? But it's beyond my strength. And, on the other hand, I cannot be a scorner.

If everything can be reduced to man and to history, I wonder where is the place: of nature—of love—of music —of art.

Revolt. We don't want just any hero whatever. The reasons for heroism are more important than the heroism itself. The value of consistency therefore precedes the value of heroism. Nietzscheian liberty is an exaltation.

Creation corrected. The character of the terrorist (Ravenel).

Relation of the absurd to revolt.[6] If the final decision is to reject suicide in order to maintain the confrontation, this amounts implicitly to admitting life as the only factual value, the one that allows the confrontation, that *is* the confrontation, "the value without which nothing." Whence it is clear that to obey that absolute value, whoever rejects suicide likewise rejects murder. Ours is the era which, having carried nihilism to its extreme conclusions, has accepted suicide. This can be verified in the ease with which we accept murder, or the justification of murder. The man who kills himself alone still maintains one value, which is the life of others. The proof is that he *never* uses the freedom and the terrible power granted him by his decision to die in order to dominate others: every suicide is illogical in some regard. But the men of the Terror have carried the values of suicide to their extreme consequence, which is legitimate murder, in other words collective suicide. Illustration: the Nazi apocalypse in 1945.

BRIANÇON. JANUARY '47

The evening that flows over these cold mountains eventually freezes the heart. I have never been able to bear this evening hour except in Provence or on the beaches of the Mediterranean.

[6] Sketch for first chapter of *The Rebel* as it appears in manuscript.

G. Orwell, *Burmese Days:*[7] "Most people can be at ease in a foreign country only when they are disparaging the inhabitants."

Id. ". . . that inordinate happiness that comes of exhaustion and achievement, and with which nothing else in life—no joy of either the body or the mind—is even able to be compared."

Read Georg Simmel (*Schopenhauer and Nietzsche*). Commentary on Nietzsche translated into English by Berneri (killed by the Communists in Spain when the Anarchists were being liquidated). Develops the longing for God in Nietzsche. "Though this may seem to us fantastic and excessive, it reveals, under the form of an extreme personalism, a feeling which, in another form, is not very distant from the Christian conception of the inner life. In Christianity, in fact, as well as our infinite distance from and smallness before God, there is the idea of becoming equal to him. The mystic of every age and every religion gives rise to this aspiration to become one with God or, more audaciously, to become God. The scholastics talk of deification, and for Meister Eckhard man can shed his human form and become God again, as he is by his proper and original nature, or, as Angelus Silesius expressed:

> I must find my ultimate end and my beginning
> I must find God in me and me in God
> And become what he is . . .

7 This quotation is from Chapter X, and the following one from Chapter XIV, of *Burmese Days* by George Orwell (1903–50), which Camus quotes in French.

This same passion was felt by Spinoza and Nietzsche: *they could not accept not being God.*"[8]

Nietzsche says: "There cannot be a God because, if there were one, I could not accept not being he."

There is but one freedom, to put oneself right with death. After that, everything is possible. I cannot force you to believe in God. Believing in God amounts to coming to terms with death. When you have accepted death, the problem of God will be solved—and not the reverse.

Radici, a member of the French militia who had volunteered for the Waffen SS, tried for having had twenty-eight prisoners in La Santé shot (he was present as the five groups were executed), belonged to the Humane Society for the Protection of Animals.

Rebatet and Morgan. On the right and the left—or universal definition of Fascism: Having no character, they adopted a doctrine.

Title for the future: System (1,500 pp.)

As human works have gradually come to cover the vast spaces where the world was asleep, to the point that the

[8] The entire passage from Simmel, including the quotation from the seventeenth-century German poet Silesius, is left in the English in which Camus reproduced it.

very idea of virgin nature now belongs to the myth of Eden (there are no more islands), peopling the deserts, subdividing the beaches, and even erasing the sky with flights of planes, leaving untouched only those regions where it so happens that man cannot live, likewise, and simultaneously (and for the same reason) the feeling for history has gradually covered the feeling for nature in the hearts of men, taking from the creator what had belonged to him and giving it to the creature. And all this through an impulse so powerful and irresistible that the day can be foreseen when silent natural creation will have yielded altogether to human creation, hideous and flashing, resounding with revolutionary and warlike clamors, humming with factories and trains, at last definitive and triumphant in the course of history—having completed its task on this earth, which was perhaps to prove that everything grandiose and staggering it could accomplish throughout thousands of years was not worth the fleeting scent of the wild rose, the olive grove, the beloved dog.

1947
Like all weak men, his decisions were brutal and unreasonably rigid.

Aesthetics of revolt. Painting makes a choice. It "isolates" and this is its way of unifying. The landscape isolates in space what is normally lost in perspective. The painting of scenes isolates in time the gesture that is normally lost in another gesture. Great painters are those who give the impression that the fixation *has just taken place* (Piero della Francesca) as if the projector had just suddenly stopped.

A play on the government of women. The men decide that they themselves have failed and that they will hand over the government to the women.

Act I — My Socrates arrives and decides to hand over the powers.

Act II — The women want to do as the men did—failure.

Act III — Under the sound advice of Socrates, they rule as women.

Act IV — Conspiracy.

Act V — They hand it back to the men.

They pretend to declare a war. "Have you realized what it means to the man who stays behind—and to see going off to slaughter all those he loves in this world?"

We can go now. We have done all that could be hoped in this world in the face of human stupidity. And what is that? A little education.

"As stupid as we but less malicious."

An experiment for a year.

If all goes well, they will be shown to the door.

All does go well but they are not shown to the door. They lacked hatred.

"It's all going to begin over again," says Socrates. They are preparing everything. Big ideas and interpretations of history. In ten years the slaughterhouses.

Listen:

A town crier

Article I — There are no more rich or poor.

Article II

"Are you going out again?"
"Yes, I have a meeting."
"I need distraction—keep my house in order."

1947
Vae mihi qui cogitare ausus sum.[9]

After a week of solitude, again keen awareness of my inadequacy for the work I have begun with the maddest of ambitions. Temptation to give it up. This long debate with a truth that is greater than I called for a more austere heart, a broader and stronger intelligence. But what can I do? I should die without that.

Revolt. Freedom in regard to death. Considering the freedom of murder, there is no freedom possible other than freedom to die; in other words, suppressing fear of death and giving that accident its place in the natural order of things. Strive toward this.

Montaigne. Change of tone in Chapter XX of Book One. On death. Amazing things he says of his fear in the face of death.

Novel — Twinkle. "When I arrived, I was exhausted by worry and fever. I went to look at the timetable to find out at what time she would get in, if by chance she was not already there. It was 11 p.m. The last train from the

9 Alas, that I ever dared to think!

west would get in at 2 a.m. I was the last to leave. She was waiting for me at the exit, alone in a group of two or three persons, with an Alsatian dog she had befriended. She came toward me. I kissed her awkwardly but I was thoroughly happy. We went out. The sky of Provence was sparkling with stars over the ramparts. She had been there since 5 p.m. She had come to meet the seven o'clock train and I wasn't on it. She was afraid that I would not come, for she had given my name at the hotel and her identification papers did not correspond. They had refused to register her and she did not dare go back there. When we reached the ramparts, she threw herself against me amid the passing crowd, which turned around to look, and hugged me with a passion which showed relief and not love but the hope of love. *I* was aware of my fever and should have liked to be strong and handsome. At the hotel, I told the truth and everything went well. But I wanted to drink a brandy before going up to our rooms. And there in the warm bar, where she made me keep drinking, I felt my confidence return and the tide of relaxation fill me completely."

His upper lip was cut lengthwise. His teeth could be seen up to the gums. So he seemed to be always laughing. But his eyes were serious.

What is man worth? What is man? All life long, after what I have seen, I shall have a suspicion and basic worry about him.

Cf. Marc Klein in *Études Germaniques:* "Observations and Reflections on the Nazi Concentration Camps."

Novel—creation corrected. "He had put the spade on the other man's neck as soon as he was on the ground. And, his foot on the spade, with the same motion that breaks clods of clay he had thrust down."

Nemesis—the goddess of measure. All those who have overstepped the limit will be pitilessly destroyed.

Isocrates: There is nothing in the universe more divine, more august, more noble than beauty.

Aeschylus, of Helen:[1] "Soul as serene as the calm of the seas, beauty that adorned the richest finery, gentle eyes piercing like an arrow, flower of love fatal to hearts."

Helen is not guilty but a victim of the gods. After the catastrophe she resumes the course of her life.

La Patellière. This moment (the final canvases) when the seasons burst forth, when mysterious hands place their flowers in every corner of the picture. A calm tragedy.

Terrorism

The great purity of the terrorist of the Kaliayev type is that for him murder coincides with suicide (cf. Savinkov: *Recollections of a Terrorist*).[2] A life is paid for by a life. The reasoning is false, but respectable. (A life taken is not worth a life given.) Today, murder by proxy. No one pays.

[1] See "Helen's Exile," in *The Myth of Sisyphus and Other Essays* (Alfred A. Knopf, 1955).
[2] Boris Savinkov (1879–1925) organized the assassination of Grand Duke Sergei in 1905.

1905, Kaliayev: sacrifice of the body. 1930: sacrifice of the mind.

PANELIER, JUNE 17, '47

Beautiful day. A frothy light, shining and soft above and around the huge beeches. It seems secreted by all the branches. The clusters of leaves stirring slowly in that blue gold like a thousand mouths with multiple lips salivating all day long this airy, golden, sweet juice—or else a thousand little contorted green bronze waterspouts ceaselessly irrigating the sky with a blue and sparkling water—or else . . . But that's enough.

How impossible it is to *say* that anyone is absolutely guilty, and hence impossible to decree total punishment.

Criticism of the idea of efficacy—a chapter.

German philosophy introduced movement into things of the reason and of the Universe—whereas the Ancients saw fixity. German philosophy will not be superseded— man will not be saved—except by defining what is fixed and what is mobile (and what we don't know whether to class as fixed or mobile).

The end of the absurd, rebellious, etc., movement, the end of the contemporary world consequently, is compassion in the original sense; in other words, ultimately love and poetry. But that calls for an innocence I no longer have.

All I can do is to recognize the way leading to it and to be receptive to the time of the innocents. To see it, at least, before dying.

Hegel against nature. Cf. *Logic*, 36–40. Why nature is abstract. What is concrete is the mind.

It is the great adventure of intelligence—the one that eventually kills everything.

To put into the archives of *The Plague:*

1) Anonymous letters denouncing families. The type of bureaucratic interrogation;

2) Types of persons arrested.[3]

Without sequel

First series. Absurd: *The Stranger* — *The Myth of Sisyphus* — *Caligula* and *The Misunderstanding*.

Second series. Revolt: *The Plague* (and annexes) — *The Rebel* — Kaliayev.

Third Series. Judgment — The First Man.

Fourth series. Love sundered: The Stake — On love — The Charmer.

Fifth series. Creation corrected or The System:[4] Big novel + great meditation + unplayable play.

JUNE 25, '47

Melancholy of success.[5] Opposition is essential. If everything were harder for me, as it was before, I should have

---

[3] Nothing like this is found either in Camus's files or in "Les Archives de la Peste" in *Cahiers de la Pléiade*, April 1947.

[4] See p. 151 of this *Notebook*.

[5] Camus received the Prix des Critiques for *La Peste*.

September 1945 – April 1948

much more right to say what I am saying. The fact remains that I can help many people—in the meantime.

Distrust of formal virtue—there is the explanation of this world. Those who have felt this distrust in regard to themselves and extended it to all others derived from it a regular susceptibility in regard to any declared virtue. Whence it is easy to come to suspect virtue *in action*. Hence they chose to call virtue whatever helps to bring about the society they desire. The deeper motive (that distrust) is noble. Whether or not the logic is sound is the question.

I too have an account to settle with that idea. Everything I have ever thought or written is related to that distrust (it is the subject of *The Stranger*). The moment I do not accept the pure and simple negation (nihilism or historical materialism) of the "virtuous conscience" as Hegel says, I have a middle term to find. Being in history while referring to values that go beyond history—is it possible, legitimate? Does not the value of ignorance itself cover a convenient refuge? Nothing is pure, nothing is pure— this is the cry that has poisoned our century.

The temptation to side with those who negate and are active! There are some who take up falsehood as one takes up a religious life. And with the same wonderful impulse, that is certain. But what is an impulse? By what, whom, why shall we judge?

If the progress of history is really this, if there is no liberation but merely unification, am I not among those who are holding up history? No liberation without unification, they say, and, if that is true, then we are falling behind. But to be out in front one must prefer a barely probable hypothesis, which has been *historically* belied in a terrifying way, to such realities as misfortune, murder, and exile for two or three generations. Hence choice depends on a hypothesis. It is not proven that liberation first calls for unification. It is not proven either that it can do without it. But there is no proof that unification must come about through violence—usually violence brings lacerating suffering under the guise of unity. It is probable that unification, liberation are necessary, possible that such unification has a chance of coming about through *knowledge* and preaching. Speech would then be an act. At least one would have to give oneself altogether to that task.

Ah! these are hours of doubt. And who can bear alone the doubt of a whole world?

I know myself too well to believe in pure virtue.

Play. The Terror. A nihilist. Violence everywhere. Everywhere falsehood.

Destroy, destroy.
A realist. He must get into the Okhrana.
Between the two, Kaliayev. — No, Boris, no.

"I love them."
"Why do you say that in such a terrible way?"
"Because my love is terrible."

Id. Yanek and Dora.
Y. gently: "And love?"
D.: "Love, Yanek? There is no love."
Y.: "Oh! Dora, how can you say that, *you* whose heart I know?"

"There is too much blood, you see, too much harsh violence. Those who love justice too much have no right to love. They are rigid like me, their heads high, their eyes unswerving. What part could love play in this proud heart? Love gently bows heads, Yanek, whereas *we* chop them off."

"But we love our people, Dora."

"Yes, we love them with a great unhappy love. But do the people love us, and do they know that we love them? The people remain silent. What silence, what silence . . ."

"But that's just what love is, Dora. To give all and to sacrifice all without hope of return."

"Perhaps, Yanek. That's pure love, eternal love. It's the kind that burns me, in fact. But at certain hours I wonder if love is not something else, if it can cease to be a monologue and if there is not sometimes a response. I imagine this, you see: heads bow gently, the heart drops its pride, eyes close and arms open a little. To forget the world's painful suffering, Yanek, to let oneself go at last, for an hour, a mere little hour of selfishness, can you imagine that?"

"Yes, Dora, that's called being in love."

"You sense everything, darling. That's called being in love. But are you in love with justice in that way?"

Yanek is silent.

"Do you love your people with that surrender or with the flame of revenge and revolt?"

Yanek is silent.

"You see. And are you in love with *me*, Yanek?"

"I love you more than anything in the world."

"More than justice?"

"I don't distinguish between you, the Organization, and justice."

"I know. But answer me. Answer me, I beg you. Yanek; answer me. Are you in love with me in solitude, with possessiveness?"

"Oh! Dora, I am dying to say yes."

"Say it, darling. Say it if you think so and if it is true. Say it in the face of the Organization, and justice, and the world's suffering, and the enslaved people! Say it, I beg you, in the face of the death agony of children and the endless prisons, despite those who are hanged and those who are beaten to death."

Yanek blanches.

"Stop, Dora. Stop!"

"Oh, Yanek! You haven't said it yet."

A silence.

"I can't say it. And yet my heart is full of you."

She laughs as if she were weeping.

"That's all right, darling. You see, it wasn't reasonable. *I* couldn't have said it either. I love you with the same rather static love, in justice and the prisons. We are not of this world, Yanek. Our share is blood and the cold rope."

Revolt is the barking of a mad dog (*Antony and Cleopatra*).

I have read over all these notebooks—beginning with the first. This was obvious to me: landscapes gradually disappear. The modern cancer is gnawing me too.

The most serious problem facing minds today: conformity.

For Lao Tse: the less one acts, the more one dominates.

G. lived with his grandmother, who sold funeral accessories in Saint-Brieuc; he did his lessons on a tombstone!

See *Crapouillot:* issue on Anarchy. Tailhade: Recollections of a prosecutor. Stirner: *The Ego and His Own.*

G. "Irony does not necessarily come from spitefulness."
M. "Most certainly, it doesn't come from kindness."
G. "No. But perhaps from suffering, of which we never think *in others.*"

In Moscow threatened by the White Army, to Lenin who decided to mobilize common-law prisoners:
"No—not *with* them."
"*For* them," Lenin said.

Kaliayev play: Impossible to kill a man in the *flesh;* one kills the tyrant. Not the fellow who shaved that morning, etc., etc.

Scene: The *agent provocateur* is executed.

The great problem of life is knowing how to slip between men.[6]

X. "I am a man who believes in nothing and loves no one, at least originally. There is a void, a frightening desert in me . . ."

[6] The manuscript has in parenthesis: A.F.

Marc condemned to death in the prison of Loos. Refuses to have his chains removed during Holy Week, the better to resemble the Savior. But there was a time when he used to shoot his revolver at crucifixes along the roads.

Happy Christians. They kept grace for themselves and left us charity.

Grenier.[7] Concerning the good use of freedom. "Modern man has ceased to believe in a God to be obeyed (Hebrew and Christian), a society to be respected (Hindu and Chinese), a nature to be followed (Greek and Roman)."

Id. "Whoever greatly loves a value is thereby an enemy of freedom. Whoever loves freedom above all either negates values or else adopts them only temporarily. (Tolerance coming from the decay of values.)"

"If we stop (on the path of negation), this is less to spare others than to spare ourselves." (No for oneself, yes for others!)

Play
D. "The sad thing, Yanek, is that all this ages us. Never again, never again shall we be children. We can die now; we have learned all about man. (Murder is the ultimate.)"

"No, Yanek, if the only solution is death, then we are not on the ʼight path. The right path is the one that leads to life."

"We have taken on ourselves the world's misfortune; this is a pride that will be punished."

[7] Jean Grenier, Camus's teacher of philosophy in Algiers, greatly influenced his thought. *The Rebel* is dedicated to him, as are other works by Camus.

"We have gone from childhood loves to that first and last mistress: death. We went too fast. We are not human beings."

Misfortune of this age. Not so long ago, bad deeds called for justification, but today it's good deeds.

Novel. "If I love her, I want her to know me for what I was. For she thinks this admirable kindness . . . But no, she is exceptional.

Reaction? If it is to take history as far back as possible, I shall never go so far as they—as far as Pharaoh.

Defoe: "I was born to destroy myself."
Id.: "I have heard of a man who, disgusted with the unbearable conversation of some of his acquaintances . . . suddenly decided never to speak again . . ." (Play)
Marion on Defoe (p. 139). Twenty-nine years of silence. His wife goes mad. His children leave. His daughter remains. Fever, delirium. He speaks. Subsequently speaks often, but little with the daughter "and very rarely with anyone else."

Psalm 91: "I will say of the Lord, He is my refuge and my fortress . . . Surely he shall deliver thee from the snare of the fowler, and from the noisome pestilence . . . Thou shalt not be afraid for the terror by night; nor for the arrow that flieth by day; nor for the pestilence that walketh in darkness; nor for the destruction that wasteth at noonday."

Utter solitude. In the urinal of a major railway station at 1 a.m.[8]

A man (a Frenchman?), a holy man who has lived his whole life in sin (never partaking of Communion, not marrying the woman with whom he lived) because, unable to endure the idea that a single soul was damned, he wanted to be damned too.

"It involved the love that is greater than all: the love of the man who gives his soul for a friend."

Merleau-Ponty.[9] Learn how to read. He complains of having been read carelessly—and misunderstood. I should have been inclined to this kind of complaint at one time. Now I know that it is not justified. There is no misunderstanding.

Profligates who are virtuous in their principles. True. But practically and for the moment I prefer a rake who kills no one to a puritan who kills everyone. And the thing that above all I have never been able to accept is a rake who wants to kill everyone.

M.P. or the typical contemporary man: the one who keeps score. He explains that no one is ever right and that it's not so easy (I hope he's not going to the trouble of proving this for my sake). But a little further on he exclaims that Hitler is a criminal and that any resistance to him will always be right. If no one is right, then one must not

[8] This remark was added in longhand to the initial typescript of the *Notebooks*.

[9] The philosopher had just published *Humanisme et terreur*, and the break between Merleau-Ponty and Camus followed that publication. (See Sartre's *Merleau-Ponty vivant*, p. 313.)

judge. But *today* one has to be against Hitler. He has kept score. He continues.

Henceforth, action seems to us justifiable only for limited objectives. So speaks the contemporary man. There is a contradiction.

Dwinger[1] (in a Siberian camp): "If we were animals, everything would have been over long ago, but we are men."

Id. A lieutenant, a pianist who lives for his art. He constructs a mute piano with boards taken from packing cases. He plays six to eight hours a day. He hears every note. In certain passages, his face lights up.

This is what we shall *all* be doing, at the end.

Id. During the phony war. In a train behind the lines, D. and a friend enter a compartment where there is a tall captain with feverish eyes. Opposite him, someone stretched out on the seat, a form covered with a cloak. Night falls. The moon lights the compartment. "Open your eyes, brothers. You will see something as a reward." He draws back the cloak slowly: a naked young woman, of great and conventional beauty . . . "Look," the officer said. "This will give you renewed strength. And you will know why we are fighting. For we are fighting for beauty too, aren't we? *Except that no one ever says so.*"

Concerning Bataille on *The Plague.*[2] Sade too called for abolition of capital punishment, of *legitimate* murder. Rea-

1 See Edwin Erich Dwinger, *Mon Journal de Sibérie* and *Entre les Rouges et les Blancs*, 1931.
2 The review of *La Peste* by Georges Bataille appeared in *Critique*, Nos. 13–14 (June–July 1947).

son: the murderer has an excuse in the passions of nature;
the law does not.

Study on G.:[3] G. as a mind opposed to Malraux. And
both of them are aware of the temptation represented by
the other mind. The world today is a dialogue between
M. and G.

Play. Yanek to another who is the Killer.
Yanek: "Perhaps. But that will deprive us of love."
The Killer: "Who says so?"
Yanek: "Dora."
The Killer: "Dora is a woman and women don't know
what love is . . . That terrible explosion in which I am going
to destroy myself is the very bursting of love."

Days of Our Death. 72 — 125 — 190.[4]
U.C. 15 — 66.

Keep the element of *breach,* of crime in violence—in
other words, recognize it only when linked to a *personal*
responsibility. Otherwise, violence is committed *on order;*
it *fits the order*—either law or metaphysics. Violence ceases
to be a breach. It escapes contradiction and represents
paradoxically a leap into comfort. *Violence has been made
comfortable.*

[3] Probably Jean Grenier.
[4] *Les Jours de notre mort* and *L'Univers concentrationnaire* (here ab-
breviated to U.C.) by David Rousset both deal with life in a concentration camp (1946).

M.D.'s friend who goes, as he does every day, to his customary little café in the rue Dauphine and sits at the same table to watch the same pinochle players. The player behind whom he sits has nothing but spades. "Too bad," M.D.'s friend says, "that you're not playing no trumps." And he dies suddenly.

Id. The elderly spiritualist who lost her son in the war: "Wherever I go, I have my son behind me."

Id. The aged colonial governor, stiff as a poker, who insists on being called "Governor." He is carrying on research to establish a table of equivalences with the Gregorian calendar. He waxes enthusiastic about only one subject, his age: "Eighty! Never an aperitif and just look!" Then he jumps up and down several times kicking himself in the behind.

Palante[5] (S.I.): "Humanism is an invasion of the priestly mind into the realm of feeling . . . It's the glacial cold of the Mind's reign."

We are blamed for making men abstract. But this is because the man who serves us as a model is abstract. We are blamed for not knowing love, but this is because (the man who serves us as a model) is incapable of love, etc., etc. . . .

Lautréamont:[6] All the water in the sea would not suffice to wash out a spot of intellectual blood.

[5] The philosopher Georges Palante was Louis Guilloux's teacher in Saint-Brieuc and a friend of Camus's professor Jean Grenier. *S.I.* stands for *La Sensibilité individualiste,* by Palante (1909).

[6] Comte de Lautréamont (1846–70) was the pseudonym of the French poet of the revolutionary *Chants de Maldoror.*

NOTEBOOK V

Short story or novel on Justice. Tortured, standing up for five days, without eating or drinking, forbidden to lean on anything, etc., etc. They come to help him escape. He refuses: he doesn't have the strength. Remaining calls for less effort. He will be tortured again and he will die.

Isle-sur-Sorgue.[7] Large room open onto autumn. Autumnal itself with its furniture made of twisted tree forms and the dead leaves of plane trees slipping into the room, driven by the wind under the windows curtained with embroidered ferns.

When R.C. leaves the Maquis in May '44 to go to North Africa, an airplane leaves the foothills of the Alps and flies over the Durance at night. And all along the mountains he sees fires lighted by his men as a sign of farewell.
At Calvi he goes to bed (invasion of dreams). In the morning he awakes and sees a terrace covered with big butts of American cigarettes. After four years of struggling and clenching his teeth, tears burst forth, and for a whole hour he weeps as he looks at the butts.

The old Communist militant who sees what he sees and can't become accustomed to it: "I can't be cured of my heart."

[7] A town of fewer than 8,000 inhabitants, Isle-sur-Sorgue stands about fifteen miles east of Avignon, hence close to Petrarch's Fontaine de Vaucluse and not far from Camus's Lourmarin. Camus's friend, the poet René Char (doubtless the R.C. referred to later), lived there.

Bayle: *Various Thoughts on the Comet.*
"One must not judge the life of a man either by what he believes or by what he publishes in his books."

The informer who keeps his accounts up to date. Several colors of ink. Strokes drawn with a ruler. The names written in a round hand.

How to make clear that a poor child may be ashamed without feeling envious?

The old beggar to Eleanor Clark: "It's not that you are a bad man, but you lose the light."[8]

Sartre or nostalgia for the universal idyll.

Ravachol (interrogation): "Before those who bring truth, facts, the welfare of humanity, all obstacles must disappear, and if subsequently there remained on earth but a few men, those at least would be happy."
Id. (Declaration to the Court): "As to the innocent victims I may have made, I regret it sincerely. I regret it particularly because my life has been full of bitterness."
Statement of a witness (Chaumartin): "He didn't love women and drank nothing but water, with a little lemon in it."

[8] See *The Fall* (Alfred A. Knopf, 1957), p. 145, for Camus's utilization of this remark.

Vigny (correspondence): "The social order is always bad; from time to time it is merely bearable. From the bad to the bearable, the dispute is not worth a drop of blood." No, the bearable deserves, if not blood, at least the effort of a whole lifetime.

Misanthropic in the group, the individualist pardons the individual.

Sainte-Beuve: "I have always thought that if one said for a single minute what one thinks, society would come toppling down."

B. Constant[9] (a prophet!): "In order to live in peace one has to take almost as much trouble as one would to govern the world."

To sacrifice oneself for humanity: according to Sainte-Beuve, one wants to play a popular role to the very end.

Stendhal: "I shall not have accomplished anything for my individual happiness so long as I am not accustomed to endure being uncomfortable in a soul."

Palante correctly says that if there is a single, universal truth, liberty has no justification.

[9] Benjamin Constant (1767–1830), the author of *Adolphe*, which Camus earlier contrasted with *La Princesse de Clèves*, was a significant figure in liberal politics during the Restoration.

October 14, '47. Time is running out. Alone and every energy tense in a dry air.

October 17. Beginning.

It is as if for man one had absolutely to choose between degradation and punishment.

At the Children's Hospital. Small, low-ceiling ward closed up and overheated—full of the smell of beef tea and surgical dressings . . . faint.

There are messianic acts and deliberate acts.

Write everything—just as it comes.

We can do everything in the way of betterment, understand everything and then dominate everything. But we shall never be able to find or to create for ourselves that strength of love which has been taken from us forever.

Capital punishment. I am made to say that I am against any violence, whatever it may be.[1] This would be as intel-

---

[1] See reply to Emmanuel d'Astier de la Vigerie in *Actuelles*.

ligent as being against the wind's always blowing in the same direction.

But no one is guilty absolutely; hence no one can be condemned absolutely. No one is guilty absolutely (1) in the eyes of society or (2) in the eyes of the individual. Something in him shares in suffering.

Is death the absolute punishment? Not for Christians. But this world is not Christian. Is not forced labor worse? (Paulhan.) I don't know. But prison leaves a chance of choosing death (unless *out of laziness* you prefer the work to be done by others). Death leaves no chance to choose prison. Finally Rochefort: "In order to ask for abolition of the death penalty, one has to be bloodthirsty."

Generation of old men. "A young man launched into the world, rich on the outside but poor within, strives in vain to substitute outer wealth for inner wealth. He wants to receive everything *from the outside,* like those old men who try to draw new strength from the breath of young girls." (Aphorisms on wisdom in life.)

Socrates kicked. "If a donkey had struck me, would I sue him?" (Diogenes Laërtius, II, 21.)

Heine (1848): "What the world seeks and hopes for now has become utterly foreign to my heart."

Courage, according to Schopenhauer, "merely the virtue of a second lieutenant."

In Book IV of *Émile,* Rousseau advocates murder (21st note) for reasons of honor.

"A slap and a flat contradiction received and put up with have civil effects that no wise man can forestall and from which no tribunal can avenge the insulted. The inadequacy of our laws gives him his independence in this regard; he is then the sole magistrate, the sole judge between the insulter and himself; he is the sole interpreter and minister of the natural law; he owes himself justice and he alone can give it . . . I am not saying that he must go out and fight, this is extravagant; I am saying that he owes himself justice and that he is the sole dispenser of it. Without so many empty edicts against duels, if I were the sovereign I guarantee that there would never be a slap or a flat contradiction given in my states, and I should do this *by a very simple means having no connection with law courts.* However that may be, Emile knows in such a case the justice he owes to himself and the example he owes to the assurance of men of honor. It is not possible for the staunchest man to keep from being insulted, but it is possible for him to keep anyone from boasting long of having insulted him."

For Schopenhauer, the objective existence of things, their "representation," is always pleasing, whereas the subjective existence, the will, is always painful.

"All things are beautiful to the eye and ugly in their being, whence the current illusion, which always strikes me, of the external unity of the life of others."

Schopenhauer: "To have fame and youth at once is too much for a mortal."

Id. "In this world, one can indeed find education, but not happiness." Hence, "to limit oneself makes one happy."

David pursues Jehovah with entreaties when his son is ill. But as soon as he is dead, he snaps his fingers and thinks no more of him.

Voltaire: "One can succeed in this world only at the point of the sword, and one dies with one's weapon in hand."

Pecherin, a Russian émigré of the nineteenth century, who became a monk abroad and exclaimed: "What a delight to hate one's native land and to long for its collapse."

The intelligentsia and the *totalitarian* interpretation of the world.

The Petrachevsky conspirators:[2] idyllic. (Emancipation of the serfs without revolutionary action—influence of George Sand.) Love of the remote and not of the nearby. "Not finding anything worthy of attachment for me, either among men or among women, I am devoting myself to the service of humanity" (Petrachevsky). (Except for Sprechner, the model of Stavrogin.)

The individualistic socialism of Belinsky. Against Hegel for the human person. Cf. the letters to Botkin: "The fate of the subject, of the individual, of the person, is more important than the fate of the whole world and the health of the Emperor of China, in other words of the Hegelian Allgemeinheit."

2 Readings for *The Just Assassins.*

Id. "I salute your philosopher's bonnet (to Hegel). But with all the respect due your philosophical philistinism, I have the honor to point out to you that if I ever reached the highest rung on the ladder of development I should then insist on an accounting of all the creatures who have been martyred by the conditions of life and of history, of all the victims of chance, of superstition, of the Inquisition, of Philip II, etc. . . . Otherwise I should hurl myself head first from that height. I do not want the happiness that is alloted to me unless I am first reassured as to each of my blood brothers, bone of my bone and flesh of my flesh. . . ."

"It is said that discord is the condition of harmony; this may be very profitable and delightful for the music lover, but certainly much less so for the one to whom is assigned the role of discord."

Petrachevsky and the idyllic ones.
Belinsky and individualistic socialism.
Dobrolyubov—ascetic, mystical, and scrupulous.
He loses his faith *when faced with evil.* (Marcion)
Chernyshevsky: "What to do?"
Pisarev: "A pair of boots is worth more than Shakespeare."
Herzen — Bakunin — Tolstoy — Dostoevsky.
The feeling of guilt among intellectuals separated from the masses. The "nobleman who repents" (of social sin).

Nechayev and the revolutionary catechism (centralized party announces bolshevism).
"The revolutionary is a marked individual. He has no interests, no business, no personal feelings, no bonds, nothing that is his alone, not even in name. Everything in him

is swallowed up by a single exclusive interest, a single thought, a single passion: Revolution."
Everything that serves the revolution is moral.
Resemblance with Dzerzhinsky, who created the Cheka.
Bakunin: "The passion for destruction is creative."
Id. Three principles of human development:
physical man
thought
revolt

The seventies. Mikhailovsky, an individualistic socialist. "If the revolutionary masses burst into my room with the intention of breaking the bust of Belinsky and destroying my library, I'd fight to the last drop of my blood."

Problem of transition. Did Russia have to pass through the stage of bourgeois and capitalist revolution, as the logic of history decreed? On this point only Tkatchev (with Nechayev and Bakunin) is the predecessor of Lenin. Marx and Engels were Mensheviks. The only thing they had in mind was the bourgeois revolution to come.

The constant discussions of the original Marxists as to the necessity of a capitalist development in Russia and their inclination to accept such a development. Tikhomirov, an old member of the party of the people's will, accuses them of making themselves "the champions of the first capitalizations."

Lermontov's prediction:

But already, bursting from vast cemeteries,
The Plague comes prowling in fatal markets.

Cf. Berdiayev, p. 107.

The spiritual communism of Dostoevsky is: the moral responsibility of all.

Berdiayev: "There can be no dialectic of matter; dialectic supposes Logos and Thought; a dialectic is possible only when of thought and mind. Marx transferred the properties of mind into the realm of matter."

In the end, it's the will of the proletariat that transforms the world. Hence there is *truly* in Marxism an existential philosophy pointing out the falsehood of objectivation and asserting the triumph of human activity.

In Russian *volia* means *both* will and freedom.

Question to be asked of Marxism:

"Is Marxist ideology the reflection of economic activity like all other ideologies, or else does it claim to discover absolute truth independent of historical forms of economy and economic interests?" In other words, is it a pragmatism or an absolute realism?

Lenin asserts the primacy of politics over economics (despite Marxism).

Lukács: The revolutionary sense is the sense of totality. Conception of the total world in which theory and practice are identified.

Religious sense, according to Berdiayev.[3]

[3] After being a Marxist, Nicolai Berdiayev (1874–1948) turned to Orthodoxy and became one of Russia's foremost religious thinkers.

What exists in Russia is a "total" collective freedom and not a personal one. But what is a total freedom? One is free *of* something—in relation to. Obviously, the limit is freedom in relation to God. You then see clearly that it means subjection to man.

Berdiayev compares Pobedonostsev (Chairman of the Holy Synod who directed the Russian Empire ideologically) and Lenin. Both *nihilists*.

Vera Figner:[4] "To harmonize words and deeds, to demand of others a harmony between words and deeds . . . this was to be my motto in life."
Id. "I considered unthinkable the formation of a secret society within an already secret society."
The Czar's budget fed 80 to 90% by the lower classes.

Every member of the "People's Will" took a solemn vow to devote his strength to the revolution, to forget for it bonds of blood, personal likes, love and friendship . . .

Play. Dora: "If you love nothing, this can't end well."

How numerous were the members of the "People's Will"? Five hundred. The Russian Empire? More than a hundred million.

[4] Here and elsewhere, Camus is doubtless referring to *Memoirs of a Revolutionist* by Vera Nicolaevna Figner.

Sofia Perovskaya, climbing the scaffold with her fellow
fighters, kisses three of them (Jeliabov, Kilbatchiche, and
Mikhailov) but not the fourth, Ryssakov, who had fought
valiantly nevertheless, but who, to save his life, had re-
vealed an address and caused the loss of three other comrades. Ryssakov is hanged and dies in solitude.

It was Ryssakov who threw the bomb at Alexander II.
Unscathed, the Czar said: "Thank God, all is well." "We
shall see if all is well," Ryssakov replied. And a second
bomb, Grinevitsky's, strikes down the Emperor.

Cf. Vera Figner, p. 190, on the denunciation.
Id. Maria Kolougnaya. Liberated, she is accused of having betrayed. In order to clear herself, she shoots at a police
officer. Condemned to prison. She commits suicide at Kara
to protest with two comrades against the corporal punishment inflicted on a third (p. 239).

To remind Christians. "Christian Fraternity." An appeal
to "all those who venerated the holy teaching of Christ."
"The present government, all the laws founded on lies, op-
pression and prohibition of the free pursuit of truth, were
to be considered as illegitimate, contrary to the divine will
and to the Christian spirit."

Vera Figner: "I had to live, live to be judged. For the trial
crowns the revolutionary's activity."

A man condemned to death: "During my whole brief life,
I have never seen anything but evil . . . In such conditions

and with such a life, can one love anything whatever, *even what is good?*"

In the eighties, a soldier who has killed a non-commissioned officer is executed. But first, turning in each direction, he exclaims: "Farewell, North. Farewell, South . . . East, West."

No one, so much as I, was so sure of conquering the world by straight means. And now . . . Where was the slip then, what weakened suddenly and determined the rest? . . .

Small fact: people often think they "have met me somewhere."

Paris–Algiers. The airplane as one of the elements of modern negation and abstraction. There is no more nature; the deep gorge, true relief, the impassable mountain stream, everything disappears. There remains *a diagram*—a map.

Man, in short, looks through the eyes of God. And he perceives then that God can have but an abstract view. This is not a good thing.

Polemics—as an element of abstraction. Every time you have decided to consider a man as an enemy, you make him abstract. You set him at a distance; you don't want to know that he has a hearty laugh. He has become a *silhouette*.

Etc., etc.

If, to outgrow nihilism, one must return to Christianity, one may well follow the impulse and outgrow Christianity in Hellenism.

Plato goes from nonsense to reason and from reason to myth. He contains all.

Glorious morning over the harbor of Algiers. The landscape, ultramarine, takes the windows by storm and spreads throughout the bedroom.

Socrates: "I have no liking for you." On his return from the camp.
End of II. He shows his marks:
"What's that?"
"Those are the marks."
"What marks?"
"The marks of men's love."

The complaints because my books do not bring out the political aspect. Translation: they want me to feature parties. But I feature only individuals, opposed to the State machine, because I know what I am saying.

The world will be more just insofar as it is more chaste (G. Sorel).[5]

5 The social philosopher of revolutionary syndicalism, Georges Sorel (1874–1922) influenced thinkers chiefly through his *Reflections on Violence.*

In the theater: necessity, for the sake of variety, to change syntactical constructions.

Play. Dora or another woman: "Condemned, condemned to be heroes and saints. Forced to be heroes. Because they don't interest us, you understand, they don't interest us at all, the filthy affairs of this poisoned, stupid world that clings to us like glue. Admit, admit it, that what interests you are human beings, and their faces. And that, claiming to seek a truth, you are really waiting only for love."

"Don't weep. This is the day of justification. Something is emerging at this moment which is the testimony of us rebels."

Novel. The man who is caught by the political police because he was too lazy to take care of the passport. He knew it. He didn't do it, etc. . . .

"I had every luxury. And here I am a slave forever . . . etc."

Rousset.[6] What silences me is that I was not deported. But I know what a cry I stifle as I say this.

It is Christianity that explains bolshevism. Let's keep the balance in order not to become murderers.

[6] David Rousset's *L'Univers concentrationnaire* (1946) depicts the horror of life in a concentration camp in Germany.

Contemporary literature. Easier to shock than to convince.

R.C. In a train during the Occupation, at daybreak. Germans. A woman drops a gold piece. C. covers it with his foot and gives it back to her. The woman: thank you. She passes him a cigarette. He accepts. She passes them to the Germans. R.C.: "On second thought, Madame, I am giving you back your cigarette." A German stares at him. Tunnel. A hand squeezes his. "I am a Pole." Out of the tunnel, R.C. looks at the German. His eyes are full of tears. In the station the German, as he leaves, turns to him and winks. C. does likewise and smiles. "Swine!" says a Frenchman who took in the scene.

Form and revolt. To give a form to what has none is the purpose of any work. Hence there is not only creation, but correction (see above). Whence importance of the *form*. Whence necessity of a style for each subject, not altogether different because the author's special language belongs to him. But it so happens that it will bring out, not the *unity* of this or that book, but the unity of the entire work.

There is no justice; there are only limits.

The Tolstoyan anarchist during the Occupation. He wrote on his door: "Wherever you come from, you are welcome." And it was the militia that came.

Dictionary. *Umanity:*[7] written with an *h* and generally executed with an axe. But here we are against . . . Derivations: *pretext.* Synonyms: Straw mattress — stepping stone — gargle — terminus.

Palinode: Exercise of lofty literature that consists in raising the flag after having spit on it, in returning to morality by way of the orgy, and in putting slippers on former pirates. One begins by playing the part of safe-cracker and ends up with the Legion of Honor. *Hist.:* 80% of the writers of the twentieth century, if only they could avoid signing, would write and honor the name of God. *Natural Sciences:* Process of transformation by which the striped insubordinate becomes the common variety of headwaiter.

Tragedy. He is *suspected* of treason. This suspicion is enough to force him to get killed. It's the only possible proof.

Leysin.[8] Snow and clouds in the valley up to the peaks. Over that motionless sea of cotton batting, the jackdaws like black gulls fly in a flock, their wings powdered with spray from the snow.

Tolstoy: "A strong west wind swept up the dust of road and fields in columns, bent the crests of the lofty lindens and birches of the garden, and carried afar the falling yellow leaves" (*Childhood*).

Id. "If it were granted me in the painful hours of life to

[7] It is unusual for Camus to indulge in such wordplay, largely lost in translation. The word for "axe" (*hache*) and the letter *h* are pronounced alike, as are the meaningless *mètre d'autel* ("altar meter") and *maître d'hôtel.*

[8] Leysin is southeast of the Lake of Geneva in Switzerland.

see again that smile (his mother's) but for a moment, I should not know pain."

I withdrew from the world not because I had enemies, but because I had friends. Not because they did me an ill turn as is customary, but because they thought me better than I am. It was a lie I could not endure.

An extreme virtue that consists in killing one's passions. A deeper virtue that consists in balancing them.

Everything worthwhile today in the contemporary spirit is located in the irrational. And yet everything that prevails in politics professes, kills, and dominates in the name of Reason.

Peace would consist of loving in silence. But there is conscience, and the person; one must speak out. Loving becomes hell.

The actor P.B., who is lazy and devout, listens to mass on the radio from his bed. He doesn't have to get up. He has done his duty.

Ludmilla Pitoëff:[9] "The audience bothers me, rather. When there is none, everything is perfect." Speaking of G.P.: "He has never ceased to surprise me."

[9] The wife of the Russian-born actor and director, Georges Pitoëff (1886–1939), here referred to as G.P., Ludmilla Pitoëff was one of the great actresses of the twenties and thirties.

According to the Egyptians, the just man must be able to say after his death: "I have not caused suffering to anyone." Otherwise, he is punished.

The conclusion is that history can achieve its ends only by means of stamping out spiritual conquests. We are reduced to this . . .

For Christians, Revelation stands at the beginning of history. For Marxists, it stands at the end. Two religions.

Little bay before Tenès, at the foot of the chains of mountains. Perfect half-circle. As evening falls, a ripeness full of anguish hangs over the silent waters. Then one realizes that if the Greeks formed the idea of despair and tragedy they always did so *through* beauty and its oppressive quality. It's a tragedy that culminates. Whereas the modern mind based its despair on ugliness and mediocrity.

What Char means probably. For the Greeks, beauty is a point of departure. For a European, it is an end, rarely achieved. I am not modern.

Truth of this age: As a result of living through great experiences, one becomes a liar. Be done with all the rest and state what I most deeply feel.

NOTEBOOK VI

At the end of the nineteenth century, Antoine Orly, a notary in Périgueux, suddenly left his home town to go to Patagonia, where he settled. He managed to become popular with the Indians of the country and through that popularity got himself named, after a few years, Emperor of Araucania. He had coins struck, issued postage stamps, and exercised all the prerogatives of a legitimate sovereign. So that the government of Chile, to which those distant lands belonged, brought him before a court of justice, which condemned him to death. His sentence was commuted to ten years in prison.

Liberated after ten years, he returned to Patagonia, where his subjects received him again as their emperor and he again consented to accept the title. But feeling himself aging, he thought of a successor and bequeathed the throne of Araucania to his son Louis Orly, who would become

emperor under the name of Louis I. But Louis Orly refused. Antoine then abdicated in favor of his nephew
Achille Orly of Périgueux, and died honored by his subjects.
But Achille I had no thought of going to his subjects. He
set himself up in Paris, assumed a position in society, and
led an expensive life there as an emperor. His resources
came from his distribution, for a fee, of posts as consul
of Araucania. His needs having increased, he also organized
collections to extend the Christian religion through the
construction of churches and cathedrals. Thus he received
a great amount of money, to such a degree that the Company of Jesus became concerned and appealed to the
Pope. Then it was seen that no church was under construction in Patagonia, and Achille I appeared before tribunals,
which condemned him. Ruined, the Emperor finished out
his life in Montparnasse, always frequenting the same
café, where it is believed that Queen Ranavalo paid him a
visit.

Any sacrifice is messianic. Prove that sacrifice can be
imagined through serious thought (in other words, not
messianic). The tragedy of equilibrium.

Modern art. They return to the object because they don't
know nature. They remake nature, and this is essential because they have forgotten it. *When this work is completed,*
the great years will begin.

"Without an unlimited freedom of the press, without an
absolute freedom of association, the domination of large

popular masses is inconceivable." (Rosa Luxemburg: *The Russian Revolution*)

Salvador de Madariaga: "Europe will return to its senses only when the word 'revolution' evokes shame and not pride. A country that boasts of its glorious revolution is as vain and absurd as a man boasting of his glorious appendicitis."

True in a sense. But subject to discussion.

Stendhal (Letter to Di Fiore, 34): "But my particular soul is a fire that suffers when it is not flaming."

Id. "Every novelist must try to make us believe in a *consuming passion* but never name it; this offends a sense of decency." (Letter to Mme Gauthier, 34).

Id. Against Goethe. "Goethe gave the devil as a friend to Doctor Faust and with such a powerful aid Faust does what we all did at the age of twenty: he seduces a shopgirl."

London. I recall London as a city of gardens where the birds used to wake me in the morning. London is the opposite, and yet my memory is correct. The flower carts in the streets. The docks, amazing.

National Gallery. Marvelous Piero and Velasquez.

Oxford. The well-kept stud-farms. The silence of Oxford. What would the world come here for?

Early morning on the coast of Scotland. Edinburgh: swans on the canals. The city around a false acropolis, mysterious and fogbound. The Athens of the North has no north. Chinese and Malays in Princess Street. It's a port town.

According to Simone Weil,[1] thoughts relating to the spirituality of labor, or to a presentiment of this, which are scattered in Rousseau, Sand, Tolstoy, Marx, Proudhon, are the only original thoughts of our time, the only ones we have not borrowed from the Greeks.

Germany: Misfortune that has bit too deep calls forth a disposition toward misfortune which forces one to push oneself and others into it.

According to Richelieu, and all else being equal, rebels are always less strong by half than the defenders of the official system. Because of a bad conscience.

Father de Foucauld, the *witness* of *Christ* among the Tuaregs, considered it natural to provide French Military Intelligence with information as to *the state of mind* of those same Tuaregs.

S.W. Contradiction between science and humanism. *No:* between the so-called modern scientific spirit and humanism. For determinism and force negate man.

[1] Camus was one of the discoverers of Simone Weil (1909–43) and her ardent spiritual humanitarianism, which made her give up a professorship to become a laborer.

"If justice cannot be obliterated from the hearts of men, it has a reality in this world. Then it is science that is wrong."

S.W. The Romans are the ones who degraded stoicism by substituting pride for virile love.

G. Greene:[2] "In a happy life the final disillusionment with human nature coincided with death. Nowadays they seemed to have a whole lifetime to get through somehow after it." . . . "You learned too much in these days before you came of age."
Id. Self-sacrifice . . . "—what a world to let such qualities go to waste!"
Id. "He (the secret agent) promised rashly, as if in a violent world you could promise anything at all, beyond the moment of speaking."
Id. "But he hadn't that particular faith. Unless people received their deserts, the world to him was chaos; he was faced with despair."

The writer condemned to *understanding*. He cannot be a killer.

Liking for prison among those who struggle. To be freed of their loyalties.

2 These passages, quoted in French, come from the first two parts of *The Confidential Agent* by Graham Greene.

Epigraph for "Le Bûcher!"[3]
"Men afflicted with a deep-rooted sorrow betray themselves when they are happy; they have a way of seizing
happiness as if they wanted to hug and stifle it through
jealousy . . ."

JULY '48—COMO

"What is a heaven devoid of our love?
We are alone with the horror of our life."

Play. Pride. Pride is born inland.

Funereal Provence.

Responsibility toward history does without responsibility
toward human beings. That is its comfort.

The stars twinkle in the same rhythm as the cicadas
drum. Music of the spheres.

C.'s friend: "We die at the age of forty from a bullet that
we shot into our heart at twenty."

We live too long.

[3] Camus planned to write a short story under this title ("The Stake").

In the *Crito* the dialogue between Socrates and the laws of Athens has a bearing on the Moscow trials.

Rock-colored butterflies.
The wind whistling through the dell makes a sound like rushing waters.
The Sorgue adorned with flowered dragnets.

Mania for virtue that shakes this age. Turning its back on skepticism which is in part humility, humanity strives to find a truth. It will relax when society has found an error that is livable.

Artists want to be saints and not artists. I am not a saint. We want universal consent and we'll not get it. So what?

Title for play: The Inquisition in Cadiz. Epigraph: "The Inquisition and Society are the two scourges of truth." Pascal.

Anguish at having increased injustice while thinking you are serving justice. Admit it at least and then discover that anguish to be greater: admit that total justice does not exist. At the end of the most terrible revolt, admit that you are nothing. That is true suffering.

The luck of my life is that I never met, loved (and disappointed) any but exceptional creatures. I have known virtue, dignity, simplicity, nobility, in *others*. Wonderful sight—and painful.

Gobineau. We are not descended from the monkey, but we are returning to him in great haste.

It's pleasure in living that disperses, suppresses concentration, cuts short any impulse toward greatness. But without pleasure in living . . . No, there is no solution. Unless it is to root oneself in a great love and to find in it the source of life without being punished with dispersion.

SEPTEMBER 1, 1948

"I am close to having completed the series of works I had planned to write ten years ago. They have brought me to the point of knowing my job. Now that I know my hand will not tremble, I shall be able to give my folly free rein." So spoke the man who knew what he was doing. At the end of it all, the stake.

Can a conscious man, Dostoevsky asks, respect himself at all?

D.: "And then if it occurs that the human advantage at times, not only may, but even must consist in desiring a detriment rather than an advantage."

"We truly live but a few hours of our lives . . ."

Night on the top of the Vaucluse. The milky way comes down into the clusters of lights in the valley. Everything is mixed up. There are villages in the sky and constellations in the mountainside.

One must encounter love before having encountered ethics. Or else one is torn.

There is not a single thing one does (one really does) for a human being that does not negate another human being. And when one cannot make up one's mind to negating human beings, this law sterilizes forever. In the final analysis, loving a human being amounts to killing all others.

I chose creation to escape crime. And their respect! There's a misunderstanding.

X.: "Do you drink coffee at night?"
"In general, never."

"Ten doses of sulphamides a day."
"Ten? Isn't that a lot?"
"You can take it or leave it."

André B. and his aunt who gave him a scarf, too heavy and too showy. As she checks every morning whether or not he is wearing it to go out, he goes and says goodbye to her in his shirt-sleeves and then quickly slips into his coat and overcoat in the vestibule before going out.

You begin by creating in solitude and think it's hard. Later on, you write and create surrounded by others. You then know that the undertaking is mad and that happiness was at the beginning.

. . . .

End of the novel. — "Man is a religious animal," he said. And on the cruel earth an inexorable rain fell.

Creation corrected: He is the only representative of this religion as old as man and everywhere he is hunted down.

I have tried with all my strength, knowing my weaknesses, to be a man of morality. Morality kills.

Hell is a special favor reserved for those who have asked for it insistently.

A man must not be judged either on what he says or on what he writes, according to Bayle. I add: or on what he does.

Bad reputations are easier to bear than good ones, for the good ones are heavy to drag along; one has to prove oneself always up to it and any lapse is looked upon as a crime. With bad reputations, a lapse is to your credit.

Gide dinner. Letters from young writers who ask if they should go on. Gide replies: "What? You can keep yourself from writing and you hesitate to do so?"

You begin by loving no one. Then you love all men as a group. Later on you love only a few, then a single woman, and finally one man alone.

Algiers after ten years. The faces which I recognize, after a hesitation, and which have aged. It's the gathering at the Guermantes house.[4] But on the scale of a city in which I get lost. There is no going backward. I am with this vast crowd steadily walking toward a hole in which all will fall on top of one another, pushed by a new crowd behind them, which itself . . .

From the airplane at night, the lights of the Balearics like flowers in the sea.

M.: "When I look happy, they are disappointed. They question me; they would like to get an admission that it is false, draw me to them, bring me back into their world. They feel betrayed."

4 Toward the end of Proust's *Remembrance of Things Past*, the narrator, returning to Parisian society after years of absence, finds his former friends almost unrecognizable when he encounters them again at a Guermantes reception.

To live is to verify.

Grenier. Not doing is acceptance of the future—but with grief in regard to the past. It's a dead man's philosophy.

Speech on *Don Juan* or *The Charterhouse of Parma.* And the constant insistence of French literature on preserving the elasticity and resistance of the individual mind.

Alexander Blok:[5]

"O, if you knew children
The dark and the cold of days to come."

and again:

"How painful it is to walk among men,
Pretend to go on existing."

and again:
"We are all unhappy. Our country has paved the way for our angers and quarrels. Each of us lives behind an impenetrable wall, despising all others. Our only real enemies are the priests, vodka, the crown, the police, hiding their faces and exciting us one against another. I shall strive to forget . . . all this mire to become a man and not a machine for hatching hatred . . .

" . . . The only things I love are art, children, and death."

[5] An idealistic Russian poet who became a herald of the Revolution, Alexander Blok (1880–1921) voiced many of the ideals of the 1905 Revolution.

Id. Faced with the ignorance and exhaustion of the poor:
"My blood is congealed with shame and despair. All is
but emptiness, spitefulness, blindness, poverty. Only a
total compassion can bring about a change . . . I react
like this because my conscience is not at rest . . . I know
what I must do: give away all my money, beg pardon of
everyone, distribute my possessions, my clothing . . . But
I cannot . . . I cannot . . ."
"O my dear, my beloved rabble!"

"What is on the confines of art cannot be loved" and yet:
"We shall all die, but art remains."

Prokosch. *The Seven Who Fled.*⁶ "Everyone hated him,
but they all coveted his sparkling smile, and he more than
suspected that all that most people really long for in their
heart of hearts, is the unattainable and fleeting glow of
personal beauty."

"Watchers; the rocks; below them the enormous plateau,
and above them the stars. Nothing if not strong, and what
they refused to condone in this place, so assiduously ob-
servant, was weakness; that is, impurity and frailty of
spirit."

". . . those who have lost, somewhere amongst the ardors
of childhood and youth, all power to love."

Wonderful p. 106.

⁶ The following six quotations come from pp. 31, 69, 99, 195, 285, and
390 of the novel by Frederic Prokosch (Harper & Brothers, 1937), which
Camus read in the 1948 translation by Rose Celli and Joan Smith. The
"wonderful p. 106" in the French edition deals with the magical power
of love and the longing for death.

"... his mother—the only creature for whom he had ever felt what might be called, not love, perhaps, but a certain loyalty of heart."

"The world, the world! They talk of war and money and starvation and injustice and all the rest. But the reality is much bigger, more profound, more terrible than these by far. Do you want to know what it is? It's this. The love for death."

"I foretell a great fire ... All will be consumed. All. Except those who have been purged and made eternal by the fire of the spirit. By love."
"What sort of love?"
"By the love that destroys. Love without appeasement or end!"

A short story that will take place on a day of yellow fog.

It's by rejecting a part of this world that the world is livable? Against *Amor fati,* man is the only animal that refuses to be what he is.

"Ah! I should indeed kill myself if I did not know that death itself is not a rest and that in the grave likewise a terrible anguish awaits us."

The judge enters the cell of the condemned man. The latter is young. He is smiling. He is asked if he wants to write anything. "Yes," he says. And he writes: "day of victory!" He is still smiling. The judge asks him if he wants anything. "Yes," the young man says. And he slaps the judge vigorously. People rush forward. The judge hesitates. A hatred as old as the world wells up. But he is motionless, an idea rising slowly in him. *Nothing can be done to him.* The other smiles and looks at him. "No," he says joyfully, "nothing can be done."

The judge at home with his wife.

"But," she says, "what did you do? Didn't you . . ."

"What?"

"That's right. Nothing can be done."

From trial to trial, the judge follows the line with hatred in his heart. With each accused, he awaits the moment of sagging and giving in. But it never happens. They are in agreement.

Then he judges with too much hatred. He deviates. He becomes heretical. He is condemned. Then a wave sweeps over him. This is freedom. He will slap the judge. Same scene. But he is not smiling and the other's face is before him. "Don't you want . . ."

He stares at the judge. "No," he says. "Let's go."

The limit of rebellious reasoning: to accept killing oneself in order to reject complicity with murder in general.

The duties of friendship help to endure the pleasures of society.

"Le Bûcher." "What struck me in that second period was the degree to which she had remained unknown to me in the first one, although she had filled and colored my life forever."

Id. "I imagined her. I knew those mornings when the image of the person met the day before and the rather hazy delights we enjoyed in the first effusions suddenly become clear and the rather haggard intoxication of the day before becomes a *solar* joy, the joy of the purest conquests."

Char. Calm block here below fallen from a dim disaster.[7]

I have two or three passions that may be judged guilty, that I consider such, and from which I am trying to cure myself through willpower. I succeed sometimes.

Max Jacob:[8] "One constructs an early experience with a powerful memory." Cultivate one's memory, dropping all else.

"Brevity and harshness are results of laziness."

"Do not scorn either insignificant people, or *important people*" (for me).

Novel. Back from the concentration camp. He arrives; he has recovered somewhat; he is out of breath, but precise. "Once and for all, I shall satisfy your curiosity. But after-

---

[7] *Calme bloc ici-bas chu d'un désastre obscur,* a line from Mallarmé's homage to Edgar Allan Poe, applies to any poet who appears suddenly like a meteor.

[8] The French poet Max Jacob (1876–1944), a cubist and precursor of Surrealism, was converted from Judaism to a strict Catholicism. He died in a concentration camp.

ward I don't want anyone to question me." There follows
a flat account.

Ex. "I got away."
The words came out harsh, without afterthoughts.
There were no overtones.
"I'd like to smoke."
First drag. He turns around and smiles.
"Excuse me," he said in the same calm, inscrutable
way.

After that, he never again talks of it. He lives in the most
ordinary way. Just one thing: he has no more relations
with his wife. Until the crisis and the explanation: "Everything human strikes me with horror."

Program, February–June.
   1) The Rope.[9]
   2) The Rebel.
Finish up the three volumes of essays:
   1) Literary essays. *Preface* — The Minotaur+Prometheus in Hades+Helen's Exile+Algerian Cities+ . . .
   2) Critical essays. *Preface* — Chamfort+Intelligence and the Scaffold+Agrippa d'Aubigné+Preface to Italian Chronicles+Commentaries on *Don Juan*+Jean Grenier.
   3) Political essays. *Preface* — Ten editorials+Intelligence and Courage+Neither Victims nor Executioners+Replies to D'Astier+Why Spain? +The Artist and Liberty.
February 18–28: Finish *The Rope*, first version.
March–April: Finish *The Rebel*, first version.
May: Essays.
June: Go over versions *The Rope* and *The Rebel*.
Rise early. Shower *before* breakfast.

9 Original title for *The Just Assassins.*

No cigarettes before noon.
Keeping stubbornly at work. It overcomes lapses.

Portraits. From under her veil, she looks out with her beautiful eyes. Calm beauty, rather a milkmaid's. She suddenly speaks and her mouth screws up into a parallelogram. She is ugly. Society woman.

You speak to him. He speaks. Suddenly, while continuing his sentence, his eyes are elsewhere, still on you by necessity but already wandering. Lady-killer.

Last words of Karl Gerhard, Himmler's former doctor (and knowing about Dachau):
"I regret that there is still injustice in this world."

To give oneself has no meaning unless one possesses oneself. — Or else, one gives oneself to escape one's own poverty. You can give only what you have. To be your own master before disarming.

X.: "It was the year of my peritonitis."
"It was just after my perforated intestine" . . . etc.
Visceral calendar.

Trial — When one thinks of the irreplaceable quality of a great heart's experience, the sum of knowledge it implies, the number of great battles fought and won against oneself and the harshness of fate, and yet three flunkies of the law courts are enough . . .

In a world that has ceased to believe in sin, the artist is responsible for the preaching. But if the priest's words carried, this is because they were fed by example. Hence the artist strives to become an example. This is why he is shot or deported, to his great distress. Besides, virtue is not learned so rapidly as the handling of a submachine gun. The fight is unequal.

After the assassination of Alexander II, address of the Executive Committee to Alexander III:

". . . Better than anyone, we understand how sad is the loss of such talents, of so much energy in the work of destruction."

". . . A peaceable battle of ideas will come to take the place of the violence that is more distasteful to us than to your servants and that we practice only by virtue of a sad necessity."

See strange deposition of Ryssakov, ready to serve as an informer in order to have his life spared. But he provides *himself* with reasons (p. 137 of "Famous Russian Trials").

Lieutenant Schmidt: "My death will crown all and, with torture added to it, my cause will be irreproachable and perfect."

G. That mouth scoured by the filthy erosion of sensual pleasure.

Revolt. Chapter on appearing (to oneself and to others). Dandyism, the motive for so many forms of action, even the revolutionary form.

So long as man has not dominated desire, he has dominated nothing. And he almost never dominates it.

Vinaver.[1] The writer is finally responsible toward society for what he does. But he must accept (and this is where he must be very modest, not at all demanding) not knowing his responsibility in advance, being ignorant *so long as he is writing* of the conditions of his commitment, taking a risk.

Essay. Introduction. Why refuse denunciation, police, etc. . . . if we are neither Christians nor Marxists? We have no value for that. Until we have found a basis for those values, we are condemned to choose the good (when we do choose it) in an unjustifiable way. Virtue will always be illegitimate until that time.

First Cycle. From my first books (*Noces*) to *La Corde* and *The Rebel*, my whole effort has been in reality to depersonalize myself (each time, in a different tone). Later on, I shall be able to speak in my own name.

[1] Michel Vinaver, the author of *Lataume* (1950) and *L'Objecteur* (1951).

Great souls interest me—and they alone. But I am not a great soul.

Preface to collection of articles.[2] "One of my regrets is having sacrificed too much to objectivity. Objectivity at times is a self-indulgence. Today things are clear and what belongs to the concentration camp, even socialism, must be called a concentration camp. In a sense, I shall never again be polite."

I strove toward objectivity, contrary to my nature. This is because I distrusted freedom.

Jeliabov, who organized the assassination of Alexander II, arrested forty-eight hours before the drama, asked to be executed at the same time as Ryssakov, who threw the bomb.

"Nothing but cowardice on the part of the government could explain not erecting one scaffold instead of two."

Zybin, the unbeatable decoder on the Okhrana, is kept in his post by the G.P.U. *Id.* Kommissarov, an organizer of pogroms on behalf of the Okhrana, goes over to the Cheka. "Go underground" (illegality).

"The acts of terrorism must be carefully organized. The party will assume the moral responsibility. That will assure the heroic fighters the necessary peace of mind."

Azev—grave number 1,466 in the cemetery of a Berlin suburb.

Several days before the attempt on Plehve's life, he warned "in general" Lopoukhin of the Okhrana and asked

[2] Draft of a preface for *Actuelles*.

for a raise.[3] He denounced the terrorists of the South to let the terrorists of Petersburg have a free hand. Plehve was killed; what Azev had said: "It's not from that direction (Guerchoum) that you have anything to fear."

Zoubatov the director. Defended the accused before a false committee of inquiry. And he made of him an informer.

Nine times out of ten the revolutionary developed a passion for his job as an informer.

The revolution of 1905 began with the strike of a Moscow printing plant where the workers were asking that periods and commas be counted as characters in evaluating piecework.

The St. Petersburg Soviet in 1905 called the strike with shouts of *Down with capital punishment.*

During the Moscow Commune, in Trubnaïa Square, in front of a building destroyed by the canons, a plate containing a piece of human flesh was exposed with a poster saying: "Give your mite for the victims."

Provocation. The Malinovsky case.[4] Cf. Laporte, pp. 175–76.

[3] In 1908 it was proved that Eugene Azef, the head of the terrorist organization who had plotted various assassinations, was also in the pay of the secret police. Vyacheslav Plehve, the reactionary Minister of the Interior under Nicholas II, was assassinated by terrorists in July 1904.
[4] Roman Malinovsky, the leader of the Bolshevik Party in the Duma, was likewise shown to be a police agent.

Interview Bourtzev—Azev in Frankfort—after the condemnation. Cf. Laporte, p. 221.

To Dimitri Bogrov, the assassin of Stolypin, is granted the favor of being hanged in white tie and tails.

End the first of June. Then travels. Intimate Journal. Force of life. Never get bogged down.

An essay on the alibi.

The whole history of Russian terrorism can be looked upon as a struggle between the intellectuals and absolutism, in the presence of the silent masses.

Novel. In the endless suffering of the camp, an instant of indescribable happiness.

In short, the Gospel is realistic, whereas people think it impossible to put into practice. It knows that man cannot be pure. But he can make the effort of recognizing his impurity; in other words, of pardoning. Criminals are always judges . . . The only ones who can condemn absolutely are those who are absolutely innocent . . . This is why God must be absolutely innocent.

Putting a person to death is suppressing his chance of perfection.

How to live without a few good reasons for despairing!

Preface. — Calling oneself a revolutionary and rejecting on the other hand the death penalty[5] (quote Tolstoy preface—that preface by Tolstoy, which I am now old enough to read with veneration, is not well enough known), the limiting of liberties, and wars, amounts to saying nothing. Hence one must declare that one is not a revolutionary— but more modestly a reformer. An uncompromising theory of reform. Finally, *and taking everything into consideration,* one may call oneself a rebel.

(You will lose your credit, I am told. "I hope so, if that's what it's made of.")

Tchaikovsky had the habit of eating papers (even quite important ones, at the Ministry of Justice, for instance) out of absentmindedness.

"In him there rose so violent a desire to create that only his tremendous ability to work was able to satisfy it." (N. Berberova)

"If that emotion of the artist that is called inspiration were never interrupted, it would be impossible to live." (Tchaikovsky)

"In moments of idleness, I am seized with the thought of never being capable of achieving perfection, with a dis-satisfaction, a self-hatred. The thought that I am good for nothing, that only my great activity mitigates my faults and raises me to the rank of man, in the deeper sense of the

[5] See *Actuelles.*

word, worries and torments me. Work is what saves me."
(Tchaikovsky)

And yet his music, most often, is mediocre.

Recruiting. Most would-be writers go toward Communism. It's the one position that allows them to look down on artists. From this point of view, it's the party of thwarted vocations. Heavy recruiting, you may imagine.

May 49. And now, forsake "the human" as they say.

I used to give myself subjects as pretexts to force myself to speak out.

Preface book of political essays. From this point of view, the last essay expresses rather well what I think, simply that modern man is obliged to be concerned with politics. I am concerned with it, in spite of myself and because, through my defects rather than through my virtues, I have never been able to refuse any of the obligations I encountered.

One cannot believe in kindness, in morality, and in disinterestedness because of psychology. But one cannot believe in evil, etc., because of history.

Novel.[6] The lovers in stone. And he knew now what he had suffered as long as that love lasted, which could not

6 Passage reinstated by the French publishers.

have been resolved unless . . . at the precise moment . . .
some heaven-sent wind had petrified them in the very
enthusiasm of their love and they were henceforth forever
fixed face to face, finally torn away from this cruel earth,
knowing nothing of the desires whirling around them and
turned toward each other as if toward the resplendent face
of the complementary love.

One never says a quarter of what one knows. Otherwise,
all would collapse. How little one says, and they are already
screaming.

When you have once seen the glow of happiness on the
face of a beloved person, you know that a man can have no
other vocation than to awaken that light on the faces surrounding him . . . and you are torn by the thought of the
unhappiness and night you cast, by the mere fact of living, in the hearts you encounter.

When the barbarians from the north had destroyed the
sweet kingdom of Provence and made of us French-
men . . .

Mounier advises me in *Esprit* to give up politics since
I have no head for it (this indeed is obvious) and to be
satisfied with the quite noble role, which would be so
charmingly appropriate to me, of sounding the alarm. But
what is a political mind? Reading *Esprit* doesn't tell me.
As to the "noble" role of sounding the alarm, it would require a spotless conscience. And the only vocation I feel in

myself is telling consciences that they are not spotless and reasons why they lack something.

J U L Y '49

See South American Journal, June to August 1949.

S E P T E M B E R '49

To finish up, give a new value to murder in order to oppose it to anonymous and cold and abstract destruction. The apology of murder from man to man is one of the stages on the path of revolt.

The sole effort of my life, the rest having been given me, and abundantly (except for fortune, which means nothing to me): to live the life of a normal man. I didn't want to be a man of the abyss. The tremendous effort did no good. Little by little, instead of succeeding ever better in my undertaking, I see the abyss coming closer.

Gheorghiu points out correctly that Christ's condemnation (and torture) was confused with that of the two thieves. The technique of the amalgam was already practiced in the year zero.

The only progress, according to G.: today ten thousand innocent men are set between two guilty men.

. . . the village façades erected by Potëmkin along the roads used by Catherine the Great as she inspected her empire.

Czapski (Inhuman Land) tells how Russian children would pour water over the bodies of German soldiers found in the snow and the next morning would use the frozen bodies as toboggans.

One must love life before loving its meaning, Dostoevsky says. Yes, and when the love of life disappears, no meaning consoles us for it.

The great Imam Ali: "The world is a decaying carcass. Whoever desires a piece of this world will live with dogs."

Stendhal: "Difference between Germans and other nations: they get excited through meditation instead of calming down. Second distinction: they long desperately to have character."

Sperber: "May God punish the devout who instead of going to church enter a revolutionary party in order to make a church of it."
Communism, skeptical fanaticism.
Speaking of a master (Grenier?): "Meeting that man has brought great happiness. Following him would have been bad; never forsaking him will be good."

Id. The death of Rosa Luxemburg: "For the others, she had been dead for twelve years. For them, she had been dying for twelve years."

"There are no isolated sacrifices. Behind each individual who sacrifices himself stand others whom he sacrifices with him without asking their opinion.

They want the good of the masses, but they don't love the masses. They love no one, not even themselves.

OCTOBER '49

Novel. "Somewhere, in a remote region of his soul, he loved them. They were really loved, but at such a distance that the word love took on a new meaning."

"He longed for two things, the first of which was absolute possession. The second was the absolute memory he wanted to leave her. Men are so well aware that love is destined for death that they work on the memory of that love as long as they live. He wanted to leave her a great idea of himself so that their love would be great, definitively. But he now knew that he was not great, that she would know it some day, sooner or later, and that, instead of the absolute memory, for him at least it would be absolute death. The victory, the only victory would be to realize that the love can be great even when the lover is not great. But he was not yet ready for such terrible modesty."

"He carried with him, deeply burned into him, the memory of her face tortured by suffering . . . It was at about that time that he lost his self-respect, which until then had always upheld him . . . She was right; he was inferior to love."

"One can love in chains, through stone walls several yards thick, etc. . . . But let a tiny part of the heart be subject to duty, and true love is impossible."

"He imagined a future of solitude and suffering. And he took a difficult pleasure in such imaginings. But this is because he fancied the suffering noble and harmonious. And in reality he thus imagined a future without suffering. But the moment pain was there, no further life was possible."

"He told her that the love of men was like this, a will and not a grace, and that he had to conquer himself. She insisted to him that this was not love."

"He had lost everything, even solitude."

"He shouted to her that this meant death for him and she did not consider herself touched. For with her lofty standards she considered it natural that he should die because he had failed."

"Everything is to be forgiven, and first of all existing. Existence always winds up by being a bad deed."

"It was that day that he lost her. The misfortune came only later, apparently. But he knew that it was that day. In order to keep her he ought never to have failed. Her standards were such that he could not commit a single mistake, reveal a single weakness. From anyone else she would have accepted it, she had accepted it and would accept it in the future. Not from him. Such are the privileges of love."

"There is an honor in love. When it is lost, love is nothing."

"I was petty before loving, just because I was sometimes tempted to consider myself great." (Stendhal, *Concerning Love*)

Keen in mind and paltry in heart. Or else his virtues were those of the mind, not of the heart. What he liked in her was the outer life, the romantic element, the play-acting.

Despair consists in not knowing one's reasons for fighting and even whether or not one must fight.

Walking in Paris: this memory: fires in the Brazilian countryside and the aromatic scent of coffee and spices. Cruel and sad evenings descending on that limitless land.

Revolt. The absurd implies an absence of choice. Living is choosing. Choosing is killing. The objection to the absurd is murder.

Guilloux. The artist's misfortune is that he is neither altogether a monk nor altogether a layman—and that he has both sorts of temptations.

The real problem of the moment: punishment.

Who can tell the anguish of the man who sided with the creature against the creator and who, losing the idea of his own innocence, and that of others, judges the creature, and himself, to be as criminal as the creator.

Monnerot. "The fecundity of a producer of ideas (he is speaking of Hegel) is proven by the multiplicity of possible *translations* (interpretations)."[7]

Of course not. That is true of an artist, absolutely false of a thinker.

Novel. Condemned to death. But the cyanide is got through to him . . . And there, in the solitude of his cell, he began to laugh. A vast feeling of well-being filled him. He was no longer walking into a wall. He had the whole night ahead of him. He was going to *be able to choose* . . . Tell himself: "Come on now," and then: "No, one moment more," and relish that moment . . . What a revenge! What a contradiction!

Lacking love, one can try to have honor. Sorry honor.

F.: Folly of basing anything on love, folly of breaking anything for love.

It's because God was jealous of our suffering that he came to die on the Cross. That strange look in the eyes which did not yet belong to him . . .

[7] Probably from *Sociologie du communisme* (1949) by Jules Monnerot.

L A T E   O C T O B E R '49. Relapse

An invalid must be clean to make people forget him, forgive him. And even then. Even his cleanliness is unusual.
It is suspect—like those excessively large rosettes that
crooks wear on their lapels.

After such a long certainty of being cured, this back-
sliding ought to crush me. It does indeed crush me. But
following on an unbroken succession of crushings, it rather
makes me laugh. In the end, I am liberated. Madness too
is a liberation.

"So sensitive that he could have touched pain with his
hands." (Amy Lowell speaking of Keats.)

Keats again: "There is no greater Sin after the seven
deadly than to flatter oneself into an idea of being a great
Poet [. . .] — how comfortable a feel it is to feel that such
a Crime must bring its heavy Penalty."[8]

"Get thee to a nunnery!" Yes indeed, for there is no
other way of possessing her than to keep anyone from possessing her. Except for God, whose advantages one can
readily endure: they don't concern the body.

[8] Camus quotes Keats in French. The first quotation may be found
in *The Letters of John Keats* (edited by M. B. Forman), Vol. I, p. 32,
and the second one, about the grave, in what is thought to be his last
letter to Fanny Brawne (Vol. II, p. 349). In that same letter (1820),
Keats writes: "Hamlet's heart was full of such Misery as mine is when
he said to Ophelia 'Go to a Nunnery, go, go!'"

If there is a soul, it is a mistake to believe that it is given us fully created. It is created here, throughout a whole life. And living is nothing else but that long and painful bringing forth. When the soul is ready, created by us and suffering, death comes along.

"I am glad there is such a thing as the grave." (Keats)

Chesterton. Justice is a mystery, not an illusion.

Apropos of Browning: the average man—just as he concerns me.

Kleist who burns his manuscripts twice . . . Piero della Francesca, blind at the end of his life . . . Ibsen at the end suffering from amnesia and relearning the alphabet . . . Courage! Courage!

Beauty, which helps in living, helps likewise in dying.

For millennia the world was like those Italian paintings of the Renaissance showing men being tortured on a cold marble floor while others were looking elsewhere with utter abstraction. The number of uninterested persons was staggering in comparison with the interested persons. What characterized history was the great number of people not interested in the suffering of others. Sometimes the uninterested ones had their turn. But they were surrounded by a general abstraction and *this* made up for *that*. Today everyone pretends to be interested. In law courts, witnesses suddenly turn around toward the one who was flagellated.

Peer Gynt tells his fellow citizens that the devil promised the crowd to imitate perfectly a pig's grunts. He appears and performs. But after the performance the criticisms were dogmatic. Some considered the voice too high and others too artful. All regretted that the effect was exaggerated. And yet the sounds heard came from a piglet that the devil was carrying under his cloak and pinching.

The end of Don Giovanni: the voices of damnation, silent until then, suddenly fill the stage of the universe. They were there, a secret crowd, more numerous than the living.

Rajk trial:[9] The idea of the objective criminal' who brings about the explosion between two aspects of man is an idea of current procedure, but *exaggerated*.

Marxism is a philosophy based on procedure, but without jurisprudence.

Worth noting: during the whole trial, Rajk leaned his head to the right, as he never did before.

[9] The trial of Rajk took place in September 1949.

Id. Those condemned to death in reality *not executed*, who live through *another life* in Siberia or elsewhere (hero of a novel).

Against capital punishment. Fichte. "System of Natural Law."

Novel (*end*). He recalled the time when he used to devour the biographies of famous men, rushing through the pages to the moment of their death. He wanted to know at that time what genius, greatness, sensitivity can use against death. But he knew now that such an intense curiosity was useless and that great lives carried no lessons for him. Genius does not know how to die. The poor woman does know.

Greatness consists in trying to be great. There is no other way. (This is why M. is a great woman.)

Wherever one wants to have slaves, one must have the most music possible. At least this is the idea of a German prince, as reported by Tolstoy.

"Obey," said Frederick of Prussia. But, as he was dying: "I am tired of ruling over slaves."

Novel. "I was looking for a way of not dying of his liberty. If I had found it then, I'd have given him back that liberty."

Gorky speaking of Tolstoy: "He is a man seeking God, not for himself but for others, so that God will leave him in peace in the desert he has chosen for himself."

Id. "I am not an orphan on earth so long as that man exists."

When John Huss was burned, a gentle little old woman was seen bringing her faggot to contribute to the fire.

Those moments when one yields to anguish as one does to physical pain: lying down, motionless, devoid of will and of future, listening only to the long twinges of pain.

To overcome? But anguish is just that, the thing to which one is never superior.

Novel. "When she was here and we used to tear each other apart, my anguish, my tears had a meaning. *She could see them.* With her gone, that anguish was empty, without a future. And true anguish is empty anguish. Suffering in her presence was a delightful happiness. But solitary, unrecognized anguish is the cup that is constantly offered us, from which we turn away obstinately, but from which we shall have to drink someday, more terrible than the day of death."

Nights of anguish leave a hangover—like other nights.

Novel. "One final word. The question is not to carry on a delightful, bitter dialogue with a beautiful image that has disappeared. The question is to destroy it in me scrupulously, implacably, to disfigure that face in order to spare my heart the desperate shock caused by memory . . ." "Kill that love, O my love."

Id. "For ten years he had not been able to enter a theater . . ."

Essay on the Sea.[1]

The desperate man has no native land. *I* knew that the sea existed and that is why I lived in the midst of this mortal time.

Thus people who love each other and are separated can live in pain. But whatever they say, they do not live in despair: they know that love exists.

People insist on confusing marriage and love on the one hand, happiness and love on the other. But there is nothing in common. This is why it happens, the lack of love being more frequent than love, that some marriages are happy.

Involuntary commitment.

Physical jealousy is in great part a judgment on oneself. Because one knows what one is capable of thinking, one fancies that *the other* is thinking in the same way.

[1] See "La Mer au plus près," in *L'Été.*

Days at sea, that life "rebellious to forgetting, rebellious to remembering," according to Stevenson.

Lambert.[2] "At present, I am saving all my pity for myself."

Guilloux: "In the end, one doesn't write to say something, but *not to say something.*"

Novel. "At the end of those exhausting sufferings, I turned toward that part of me that loves no one and sought refuge there. There I caught my breath. Then I returned, with head lowered, into the thickets and the thorns."

Virtue is meritorious today. Great sacrifices are not backed up. Martyrs are forgotten. They rise up and all eyes are on them. Once they have fallen, the newspapers go on.

Merle, a blackmailing journalist, got nothing from X., whom he libeled from one year to the other in his paper. Merle, changing tactics, praised outrageously his victim, who paid up at once.

Tolstoy in the Chibunin affair pleaded in court for the defendant, guilty of having struck his captain; made an appeal for him after the death sentence; wrote to his aunt to ask her to influence the Minister of War. The latter

2 E. Lambert, a friend of Jean Grenier.

pointed out only that Tolstoy had forgotten to give the address of the regiment, and this kept him from intervening. The day after Tolstoy received the letter asking him to fill in that omission, Chibunin was executed *through Tolstoy's fault.*

The last work of Tolstoy, which was found unfinished on his worktable: *"In the world, there are no guilty."*

He was born in 1828. He wrote *War and Peace* between 1863 and 1869. Between the ages of thirty-five and forty-one.

Life is too long, according to Greene.[3] "Couldn't we have committed our first major sin at seven, have ruined ourselves for love or hate at ten, have clutched at redemption on a fifteen-year-old death-bed?"

Scobie, an adulterer. "Virtue, the good life, tempted him in the dark like a sin."

Id. "In human love there is never such a thing as victory: only a few minor tactical successes before the final defeat of death or indifference."

Id. "Love was the wish to understand, and presently with constant failure the wish died too perhaps or changed into this painful affection, loyalty, pity. . . ."

Marie Dorval[4] to Vigny: "You don't know me! You don't know me!"

[3] This second group of passages from Graham Greene, quoted in French, comes from *The Heart of the Matter* (1948).

[4] The actress Marie Dorval (1798–1849), who played the great heroines of French Romantic drama, had a long liaison with the poet Alfred de Vigny.

After so much absence, no longer recognizing herself: "Is it true, tell me, that physical pleasure can make me cry out?"

Her passport delivered by Toulouse: "Figure misshapen, hair thin, glorious bearing."

"I did not separate from M. de Vigny, but tore myself away!"

Christ agonizes now in law courts. The knout in his hand, he holds sway in the teller's cages of banks.

Strepto—40 grams from November 6 to December 5, '49.
P.A.S.—360 grams from November 6 to December 5, '49.
+20 grams Strepto from November 13 to January 2.[5]

Novel. "As a result of questioning him as to his love, as a result especially of the anguish she put into that interrogation, he felt doubts coming into being. And as the doubts gradually increased, his will to love hardened. Hence, the more she appealed to his heart, the more abstract his love became."

Any murder to be justified must be balanced with love. For the terrorists the scaffold was the final proof of love.

In 1843, the Americans liberate Hawaii, which the English had had granted to them through force. Melville

5 Streptomycin and Para-Aminosalicylic Acid (or familiarly P.A.S.) are two medicaments used in the modern treatment of tuberculosis. Camus took the customary doses.

present. The king invites his subjects "to celebrate their happiness by ceasing to observe any moral, legal, or religious restraint for ten consecutive days"; during that period, he solemnly declared, all the laws of the territory were suspended.[6]

Mistakes are joyful, truth infernal.

That sacred uncertainty, of which Melville speaks, which always keeps men and nations in suspense.

Melville's note on the margins of Shelley's Essays: "Milton's Satan is morally very superior to his God, as whoever perseveres despite adversity and torture is superior to whoever, in the cold assurance of an unquestioned triumph, takes the most horrible revenge on his enemies."

Bitter are the waters of death . . .

Melville at the age of thirty-five: I have given my consent to annihilation.

Hawthorne speaking of Melville: "He can neither believe nor be comforted in his unbelief."

[6] Camus had obviously been reading *Herman Melville* by Pierre Frédérix (Gallimard, 1950), which records (pp. 122–3) this incident as related in a postscript to *Typee*. The other references to Melville derive from the same reading.

L.G. — rather beautiful, but who, as Stendhal says, leaves something to be desired for ideas.

The day he separated from his wife, he had a great longing for chocolate and succumbed to it.

The story of M. de Bocquandé's grandfather. At school he is accused of an impropriety. He denies it. Locked up for three days. He denies it. "I cannot confess a wrong I didn't do." The father is informed. He gives his son three days to confess. Otherwise he will be a cabin boy (the family is rich). Locked up for three days. He comes out. "I cannot confess what I haven't done." The father, inflexible, sends him to sea as a cabin boy. The child grows up, spends his life at sea, becomes a captain. The father dies. He grows old. And on his death bed: "It was not I."

During the Liberation of Paris, bullets whistle. "Ah! Ah!" Gaston Gallimard exclaims. Robert Gallimard rushes toward him, frantic. But Gaston merely sneezes.

She gave him pleasures of vanity. And this is why he was faithful to her.

F.: "I am a twisted person. The only way I can know my capacity for love is from my capacity for anguish. Before suffering, I don't know."

Preface to *L'Envers et l'endroit*.[7]

"There are in me artistic vetoes, as in others there are moral or religious vetoes. The forbidden, the idea that a certain thing "isn't done," which is foreign to me as a child of a free nature, belongs to me as a slave (and an admiring slave) of a rigorous artistic tradition. (I overcame such taboos only in *State of Siege*, and this explains the affection I feel for that work, generally scorned.)

". . . Perhaps also that distrust is aimed at my basic anarchy and thereby is useful. I know my disorder, the violence of certain instincts, the graceless surrender into which I can fall. The work of art to be erected (I am speaking in the future) must use those incalculable forces of man. But not without surrounding them with barriers. My barriers even today are too strong. But what they had to contain was strong too. On the day when balance is established, I shall try to write the work of which I am dreaming. It will be like *L'Envers et l'endroit;* in other words, a certain form of love will be my guiding support.

"It seems to me that I can do it. The breadth of my experiences, my professional knowledge, my violence and my submission . . . I shall set in the center, as here, a mother's wonderful silence, a man's quest to recover a love resembling that silence, finding it at last, losing it, and returning through wars, the folly of justice, pain, toward the solitary and calm, the death of which is a happy silence. I shall set . . ."

Maritain. Rebellious atheism (absolute atheism) puts history in the place of God and substitutes for revolt an absolute submission. "Duty and virtue are for it but a total

[7] Written in 1935–36 and originally published in Algiers in 1937, Camus's first book, *L'Envers et l'endroit*, was finally reissued in Paris with a long preface in 1958.

submission and a total immolation of itself to the sacred voracity of growth."

"Sanctity likewise is a revolt: it is refusing things as they are. It is taking on oneself the world's misfortune."

Publicity blurb for *The Just Assassins:* Terror and justice.

Novel. "She had a way of repeating three times 'I love you' in a whispered, breathless voice, like a rather subversive credo . . .'"

"My chief occupation despite appearances has always been love (its pleasures for a long time and, finally, its most painful transports). I have a romantic soul and have always had considerable trouble interesting it in something else."

In the spring when all is over write *everything I feel.* Little things at random.

Novel. "With most women, he had been able to pretend, victoriously. With her, never. A sort of intuition like genius made her aware of what was going through his heart, looked through him."

Criticism of *The Just Assassins:* "No idea of love." If I were so unfortunate as not to know love and wanted to put myself in the ridiculous position of learning about it, I'd not turn to Paris or the gazettes to study it.

The end of a cold day, twilights of shadows and ice . . . more than I can bear.

Preface to Political Essays: "Upon the fall of Napoleon the author of the following pages, who considered it a deception to spend his youth in political hatreds, began to travel." (Stendhal, *Life of Rossini*)

Id. Stendhal (*Concerning Love*): "Man is not free not to do what causes him more pleasure than all other possible acts."

Id. "Exceptionally beautiful women astonish less the second day. This is a great misfortune . . . etc."

The Duke of Policastro, who "every six months traveled a hundred leagues to see for a quarter of an hour in Lecca an adored mistress, who was guarded by a jealous husband." Cf. Story of Dona Diana. End of scene theater (Garnier, p. 108).

When all is over: write a hodgepodge. Everything that goes through my head.

Revolt: the end of revolt without God is philanthropy. The end of philanthrophy is trials. Chap. The Philanthropists.

An atheist when he was a model husband, he was converted when he became an adulterer.

Poor and free rather than rich and enslaved. Of course, men want to be both rich and free, and this is what leads them at times to be poor and enslaved.

Delacroix. "The illusions I create with my painting are the most real thing in me. The rest is shifting sand."

Mogador.

Delacroix: "What makes men of genius . . . is not new ideas; it is that dominant idea that what has been said has not yet been said enough."

Id. "The appearance of that region (Morocco) will always remain in my eyes. The men of that strong race will always, so long as I live, be active in my memory. It was in them that I truly encountered the beauty of the ancients."

Id. ". . . They are closer to nature in a thousand ways: their clothing, the form of their shoes. Consequently beauty is joined to everything they do. We in our corsets, our narrow shoes, our ridiculous sheaths, are an object of pity. Grace takes revenge on our learning."

Vol. I, pp. 212–13 (Plon), wonderful pages on talent

He classifies Goethe (with reasonable justification for his judgment) "among petty minds tainted with affectation."

"That man who always sees himself doing . . ."

JANUARY 10, 1950

I have never seen very clearly into myself in the final analysis. But I have always instinctively followed an invisible star . . .

There is in me an anarchy, a frightful disorder. Creating costs me a thousand deaths, for it involves an order and my whole being rebels against order. But without it I should die scattered.

In the afternoon, the sun and light flood my room, the blue and veiled sky, sounds of children rising from the village, the song of the fountain in the garden . . . and hours in Algiers come back to me. Twenty years ago . . .

L. speaking of mother: "It's bread, and what bread!"

Bespaloff:[8] "From revolt to revolt, from revolution to

8Rachel Bespaloff is a French critic of penetrating and original mind.

revolution, people thought they were increasing freedom and they landed in the Empire."

Revolt. Achilles defying creation after the death of Patroclus.

Chap. We Nietzscheans.

Henry Miller: "I am dazzled by the glorious collapse of the world."[9] But there is a kind of mind that is not dazzled by that collapse. More sordid than grandiose.

To dominate the work without forgetting *boldness*. To create.

Couvreux. Arrives, asks one to be kind enough to turn on the radio to the news broadcast of the BBC which in his opinion is always interesting, sits down, and falls asleep.

Family. "You shouldn't have disturbed yourself."
"You are going out of your way."
"He comes from inland."

Themes. Provincial hotel. Attraction of creatures.

9 "Third or Fourth Day of Spring" in *Black Spring*.

Sea. Injustice of the climate. Trees in blossom at Saint-
Étienne. Even more frightful. In the end, I should have
wanted an absolutely black face. Thus the nations of the
North . . .

FEBRUARY 1950

Disciplined work until April. Then work enthusiastically.
Be silent. Listen. Let it overflow.

The notion (and the reality) of the intellectual dates
from the eighteenth century.

Later write essay, without hesitation or reservation, *on
what I know to be true.* (Do what one doesn't want, want
what one doesn't do.)

The original night.

I am reading the life of Rachel.[1] Always the same dis-
appointment in the face of history. All those words uttered
by her, among friends for instance, which go back to the
staggering host of lost words that no one will ever know.
Compared with that host, what history records is a drop
of water lost in the sea.

In Delacroix's diary, one remark (at second hand) on
critics who indulge in creating: "One can't at one and the
same time hold the stirrups and show one's rear."

[1] Mlle Rachel (1820–58), as the great French actress was called,
distinguished herself in the roles of classical tragedy.

Delacroix—on distances in London.

"One must count in leagues: that disproportion alone
between the vastness of the place inhabited by Londoners
and the natural limitation of human proportions makes me
declare them enemies of true civilization which brings together the men of the civilization of Attica who constructed
the Parthenon as big as one of our houses and enclosed so
much intelligence, life, strength, grandeur in the narrow
limits of frontiers that raise a smile in our barbarism, so
cramped in its vast states."

Delacroix: "In music *as probably in all the other arts*
the moment that style, character, seriousness in brief,
comes to state itself, the rest disappears."

Id. What revolutions have destroyed in the realm of
monuments and works of art—when itemized, Delacroix
says, it is frightening.

Against progress. Vol. I, p. 428: "We owe to antiquity the
little we are worth."

Delacroix.

The great artist must learn to avoid *what must not be
attempted.* "Only fools and the impotent torture themselves
over the impossible. And yet *one must be very daring."*

Id. "It requires great daring to dare to *be oneself."*

Id. "To work is not solely to produce; it is to give value
to time."

Id. "The satisfaction of the man who has worked and
suitably employed his day is tremendous. When I am in

that state I enjoy delightfully the slightest distractions. I can even, without the least regret, find myself surrounded by the most boring people."

Id. ". . . not so much cling to the pursuit of things which are empty wind but enjoy work itself and the delightful hours that follow it . . ."

Id. "How happy I am no longer to be obliged to be happy in the old way (the passions)."

The great Italian schools "in which naïveté is joined to the greatest learning."

Id. Speaking of Millet: "He belongs indeed to the squad of bearded artists who brought about the revolution of '48 or applauded it, apparently thinking there would be equality in talents together with equality in fortunes."

Id. Against progress, the whole of p. 200: ". . . What a noble sight in the best of centuries, this human livestock fattened by the *philosophes*."

Id. Russian novels "have an amazing smell of reality."

P. 341: ". . . imperfect Creation . . ."

Original talent "shyness and dryness in the beginning, breadth and neglect of details in the end."

The peasant who had remained indifferent during a prayer that had drawn tears from everyone. He told the people who criticized his coldness that he didn't belong to the parish.

FEBRUARY '50

Memory slipping more and more. Ought to make up my mind to keep a diary. Delacroix is right: all these days that are not noted down are like days that didn't exist. Perhaps in April, when I shall recover my freedom.

Volume: questions of art—in which I shall sum up my aesthetics.

Literary society. One imagines black intrigues, vast ambitious schemings. There are nothing but vanities, satisfied with small rewards.

A little pride helps to maintain one's distance. Do not forget it *despite everything*.

The pleasure that winds up in gratitude: crown of days. But at the other extremity: bitter pleasure.

The *mistral* has scraped the sky down to a new skin, blue and shiny like the sea. From everywhere birds burst into song, with an exuberance, a jubilation, a joyful discord, an infinite delight. The day brims over and is aglow.

Not morality but fulfillment. And there is no other fulfillment than that of love, in other words of yielding to oneself and dying to the world. Go all the way. *Disappear*. Dissolve in love. Then the force of love will create without me. Be swallowed up. Break up. Vanish in fulfillment and the passion of truth.

Epigraph: "Nothing avails against humble, ignorant, headstrong life" (*L'Échange*).[2]

2 Both this and the following quotation are from Act III of Claudel's early play, *L'Échange*.

Id. "There was a way of loving you and I did not love you that way."

Adolphe. Rereading. Same feeling of ardent desiccation.
"She was examined (E) with interest and curiosity like a beautiful storm."
"That heart (A) foreign to every interest in the world."[3]

"The moment I saw on her face an expression of pain, her will became mine: I was at my ease only when she was satisfied with me."

". . . Those two wretched creatures who were known solely to each other on earth, who were the only ones capable of doing each other justice, of understanding and consoling each other, seemed two irreconcilable enemies, bent on tearing each other apart."

Wagner, music of slaves.

Novel. "He was quite willing that she should suffer, but far from him. He was a coward."

Constant: "One must study men's woes but count among those woes the ideas they have of the means of combatting them."

---

[3] E stands for Ellénore, the heroine, and A for Adolphe, the hero.

Id. "Frightful danger: that the American politics of business and the flabby civilization of the intellectuals should join forces."

Title for solar essays:[4] Summer. Noon. Holiday.

FEBRUARY '50

Mastery: Not to talk.

Worth noting: experience is a memory, but the reverse is true.

Return now to the detail. Prefer truth to everything.

Nietzsche: *I was ashamed of that deceptive modesty.*

The rosemary is in blossom. At the base of the olive trees, crowns of violets.

MARCH '50

Philanthropic Calvinists negate whatever is not reason because reason, to their way of thinking, can make them masters of all, even of nature. Of all except Beauty. Beauty eludes such a scheme. This is why it is so hard for an artist to be a revolutionary, even though he is a rebel as an artist. This is why it is impossible for him to be a killer.

---

4 The manuscript reads "Mediterranean Essays," which the author changed on the first typescript. Although the final title was *L'Été* (Summer), Camus continues to use *La Fête* (Holiday) in the *Notebooks.*

Wait, wait until are snuffed out one by one the days still ahead of me in a lighted garland. The last is finally snuffed out and it's utter blackness.

MARCH I

A month of absolute mastery—on every plane. Begin again anew—(but without sacrificing *the truth, the reality* of the prior experiences, and accepting all the *consequences* with the *decision* to dominate them and to transfigure them in the ultimate, but experienced, attitude of the creator. Reject nothing).

(Be able to say: it was hard. I didn't succeed the first time and I struggled at great length. But in the end I won out. And such great exhaustion makes the success more lucid, more humble, but also more determined.)

Revolt. After having written it all up, rethink the whole thing *starting with* the documents and ideas put in this order.

In art, the absolute realist would be the absolute divinity. This is why attempts to deify man aim to perfect realism.

The sea: I didn't lose myself in it; I found myself in it.

Vivet's friend, who had given up smoking, goes back to smoking on learning that the H-bomb has just been discovered.

Family.

It was the carters who made Algeria.

Michel. Eighty years old. Erect and strong.

X., his daughter. Left them at the age of eighteen to "make her own life." Returned at twenty-one full of money and, selling her jewels, rebuilt her father's stables, wiped out by an epidemic.

Gurdjieff's "astute man." Concentration. Recall of oneself (see oneself through the eyes of another).

Jacob Genns, the dictator of the Vilna ghetto, accepted that police job in order to limit the damage. Little by little, three quarters of the ghetto (48,000) are exterminated. Finally he is shot himself. Shot for nothing—dishonored for nothing.

Title: The Shrewd Genius.

She had to die. Then an atrocious happiness would begin. But that's just what anguish is: "they" don't die at the right moment.

According to the Chinese, empires on the point of collapse have very many laws.

Radiant light. It seems to me that I am emerging from a ten-year sleep—still entangled in the wrappings of misfortune and of false ethics—but again naked and attracted toward the sun. Strength brilliant and measured—and intelligence frugal, sharpened. I am being reborn as a body too . . .

Comedy. A man who is rewarded officially for a virtue he has been practicing instinctively. From that moment on, he practices it consciously: catastrophes.

The style of the seventeenth century according to Nietzsche: clean, precise, and free.
Modern art: the art of tyrannizing.

After a certain age, quarrels between individuals are aggravated by a race against time. Insoluble then.

As if at the first warmth of love the snows accumulated in her melted gradually to give way to the irresistible, gushing waters of joy.

MARCH 4, 1950

And openly I pledged my heart to the grave and suffering earth, and often in the sacred night I promised to love it faithfully unto death, without fear, with its heavy load of fatality, and to despise none of its enigmas. Thus I bound myself to it with a mortal bond. (Hölderlin's *Empedocles*)

It is only too late that one has the courage of one's knowledge.

Artists and thoughts *without sunlight.*

"Misunderstanding about affection," Nietzsche says. "A servile affection that submits and grovels, that idealizes and makes mistakes—but a divine affection that scorns and loves, that transforms and uplifts what it loves."

The world in which I am most *at ease:* the Greek myth.

The heart is not all. It *must be,* for without it . . . But it must be mastered and transfigured.

My whole work is ironic.

My most constant temptation, the one against which I have never ceased fighting to the point of exhaustion: cynicism.

Paganism for oneself, Christianity for others is the instinctive desire of each person.

Not difficulty, but impossibility of being.

Love is injustice, but justice is not enough.

There is always in man an element that rejects love. It's the element that *wants* to die. It's what asks to be forgiven.

Title for "Le Bûcher": Deianira.

Deianira. "I should have liked to catch her in time, on that already remote day in the Tuileries when she came toward me in her black skirt, with her white blouse rolled up on her tanned arms, her hair loose, her narrow foot, and her face like the prow of a ship."

"What I had long been thinking of asking her I did ask on that final evening: the oath that she would never belong to any other man. What religion can allow—I did not want to go on living if human love was incapable of the same thing. She then made me that promise without asking me to commit myself. But in the terrible joy and the pride of my love I promised it to her, joyfully. It was a matter of killing her, and killing myself, in a certain way."

Where love is a luxury, how can freedom fail to be a luxury? One more reason, to be sure, for not yielding to those who make a double woe of love and of freedom.

Voltaire suspected almost everything. He settled but very few things, yet thoroughly.

Novel. Male characters: Pierre G., Maurice Adrey, Nicholas Lazarevitch, Robert Chatté, M.D.B., Jean Grenier, Pascal Pia, Ravanel, Herrand, Oettly.

Female characters: Renée Audibert, Simone C., Suzanne O., Christiane Galindo, Blanche Balain, Lucette, Marcelle Rouchon, Simone M. B., Yvonne, Carmen, Marcelle, Charlotte, Laure, Madeleine Blanchoud, Janine, Jacqueline, Victoria, Violante, Françoise 1 and 2, Vauquelin, Leibowitz, Michèle, André Clément. Lorette, Patricia Blake, M. Thérèse, Gisèle Lazare, Renée Thomasset, Evelyne, Mamaine, Odile, Wanda, Nicole Algan, Odette Campana, Yvette Petitjean, Suzanne Agnély, Vivette, Nathalie, Virginie, Catherine, Mette, Anne.

"The sea and the sky attract to the marble terraces the crowd of young, hardy roses." A. Rimbaud.

Those who write obscurely have great luck: they will have commentators. The others will have only readers, and this, it seems, is worthy of scorn.

Gide comes to the U.S.S.R. because he thinks *of joy*.

Gide: Atheism alone can pacify the world today (!).

Dialogue between Lenin and an inmate of a Russian concentration camp.

Paris begins by serving a work of art and pushes it. But once it is established, then the fun begins. It is essential to destroy it. Thus there are in Paris as in certain streams in Brazil thousands of little fish whose job this is.[5] They are tiny, but innumerable. Their whole head, if I may say so, is in their teeth. And they completely remove the flesh from a man in five minutes, leaving nothing but the bare bones. Then they go away, sleep a little, and begin again.

From Bossuet: "The only character that most men are capable of is to object if that character is refused them." *He* had even lost that character.

Like those elderly people who, in a big house that once was full of life and voices, withdraw to a single floor, then to a single room, and then to the smallest room of all, where they bring together every aspect of life—cloistered and ready for the narrow hole in the ground, even more restricted.

APRIL '50. Cabris again.[6]

After all, one gets there. It's hard, but one eventually gets there. Ah! they're not much to see. But one forgives them. As to the two or three persons I love, they are better than I. How can I accept that? Come now, let's skip it.

[5] The same image is found in *The Fall* (Alfred A. Knopf, 1957), p. 7.
[6] Cabris, where Camus went to rest, is a mile or two from Grasse in the Alpes-Maritimes.

Foggy, warm night. In the distance, the lights along the coast. In the valley, a vast concert of toads, whose voice, at first melodious, seems to grow hoarse. Those villages of light, houses . . . "You are a poet and I am on the path of death."

A.'s suicide. Completely upset because I liked him greatly, to be sure, but also because I suddenly realized that I had a longing to do as he did.

Women at least do not have, as we do, the obligation of nobility. For men, even faith, even humility are a test of nobility. Deadly.

There always comes a moment when people give up struggling and tearing each other apart, willing at last to like each other for what they are. It's the kingdom of heaven.

Enough of guilt—of repentance.

Claudel. That greedy old man flinging himself at the Communion table to gobble up honors . . . Alas!

Short story. A good day. The middle-aged lady who arrives alone. Cannes.

In big novel. Lazarevitch. Adrey. Chatté (and his pretences with strangers).

To grow old is to move from passion to compassion.

The lady who takes calcium phosphate. At the table. "This poor dog (a beautiful flame-colored spaniel), after all the brave deeds he performed in Indochina, do you think he was decorated? Not at all; it seems that in France dogs are not decorated. But in England they are decorated when they have a war record. But here! It didn't matter that he pointed out all the ambushes of those Chinese; he didn't get a thing. Poor dog!"

The tart who frequents bars. "Mail? Not on your life! *I* don't like problems."

The nineteenth century is the century of revolt. Why? Because it was born of a thwarted revolution in which nothing but the divine principle received a fatal blow.

MAY 27, 1950

Solitary. And the fires of love set the world on fire. That is worth the pain of being born and growing up. But must one go on living, afterward? Then any life would be justified. But any afterlife?

After *The Rebel*, free creation.

How many nights in a life where one has ceased to be!

My work during these first two cycles: persons without lies, hence not real. They are not of this world. This is probably why up to now I am not a novelist in the usual sense. But rather an artist who creates myths to fit his passion and his anguish. This is also why the persons who have meant much to me in this world are always those who had the force and exclusiveness of those myths.

The mad thing about love is that one wants to hurry and *lose* the interim. In this way one wants to get closer to the end. In this way love in one of its aspects coincides with death.

Camp. An ignorant guard who takes it out on an intellectual. "Take that for your books! So you are intelligent . . ." etc. In the end the intellectual begs to be forgiven.

Men have the difficult face of their knowledge (those faces one occasionally encounters, which know). But at times under the scars there still appears the face of the adolescent, which gives thanks to life.

In their company it is not poverty, or destitution, or humiliation that I felt. Why not say it? I felt and I still feel my nobility. In the presence of my mother, I feel that I belong to a noble race: the one that envies nothing.

I lived, without restraint, on beauty: eternal bread.

For most men, war is the end of solitude. For me it is the definitive solitude.

Swift as lightning, a single, dazzling dagger thrust, the bull's copulation is chaste. It's the copulation of a god. Not enjoyment, but a burning flame and sacred annihilation.

Vosges.[7] Thanks to the red sandstone, the churches and calvaries are the color of dried blood. All the blood of conquests and of power flowed over this land and dried on its sanctuaries.

Useless ethics: life is ethical. Whoever does not give all does not obtain all.

When one has the luck to live in the universe of the intelligence, what a folly to long for the terrible world of violence and passion.

I love all or I love nothing. Hence it is that I love nothing.

End of Deianira. He kills her carefully and gradually (she was gradually disappearing before his eyes and he

[7] Camus continued his convalescence in the Vosges Mountains during the summer of 1950.

watched her features dry up, with a frightful hope and a painful sob of love). She dies. He recovers the other woman, again young and beautiful. A delightful love rose again in his heart. "I love you," he told her.

Spiritual exercises of St. Ignatius—to forestall somnolence in prayer.

All the power of knowledge today aims at strengthening the State. Not a single scholar has thought of applying his research to the defense of the individual. Yet that is where a freemasonry would have a meaning.

If our era were merely tragic! But it is revolting. This is why it must be brought to trial—and forgiven.

I. The Myth of Sisyphus (absurd) — II. The Myth of Prometheus (revolt) — III. The Myth of Nemesis.

J. de Maistre: "I don't know what the soul of a scoundrel is like, but I think I know what the soul of a respectable man is like, and it's enough to make one shudder."

Throw open the prisons or prove your virtue.

Maistre: "Woe to the generations that speak to the epochs of the world." Like that Chinese sage who, when he wished someone ill, expressed the wish that he would live in an "interesting" epoch.

Baudelaire. The world has acquired such a thick veneer of vulgarity that it confers on the spiritual man's scorn the violence[8] of a passion.

Unterlinden. "All my life I have dreamed of the peace of the cloister." (And probably I could not have put up with it more than a month.)

Europe of the shopkeeper. Heartbreaking.

Commitment. I have the loftiest idea, and the most passionate one, of art. Much too lofty to agree to subject it to anything. Much too passionate to want to divorce it from anything.

"For him love was impossible. He was entitled only to lies and adultery."

Claudel. Vulgar mind.

SAVOIE. SEPTEMBER '50

People who, like M., are eternal emigrants seeking a home eventually find it, but only in suffering.

Suffering and its often ugly face. But one must live in it and off it in order to pay the price. Destroy oneself in suffering because of having dared destroy others.

[8] The word in the manuscript might be either *violence* or *noblesse* ("nobility").

Novel. "He recalled that one day, in one of those painful scenes, while the feeling of a frightful future was growing in him, she told him she had sworn never to belong to anyone else, and that, with him gone, there would never be anyone else. And just as she thought she was sealing their love in the most irremediable way, as she was doing so indeed, just as she thought she was binding him and fusing him with her, the thought came to him on the other hand that he was liberated, that it was time to flee and leave her, sure of her absolute fidelity and sterility. But he remained that day—as he was accustomed."

PARIS. SEPTEMBER '50

What I have to say is more important that what I am. Step aside and *push aside*.

Progress: to avoid telling a beloved person of the anguish he brings us.

The fear of suffering.

Faulkner. To the question: What do you think of the young generation of writers, he replies: It will leave nothing behind. It has nothing more to say. In order to write, one must have the basic truths deeply rooted in one and have centered one's work on one of them or all at once. Those who don't know how to speak of pride, of honor, of suffering are inconsequential and their work will die with them or before they die. Goethe and Shakespeare resisted everything because they believed in the human

heart. Balzac and Flaubert likewise. They are eternal.
"What is the reason for the nihilism that has invaded writing?"

"Fear. The moment men cease being afraid, they will begin again writing masterpieces, in other words lasting works."

Sorel: "Disciples call upon their master to close the epoch of doubts by contributing definitive solutions."

There is no doubt that every ethic requires *a little* cynicism. Where is the limit?

Pascal: "I spent a great part of my life in the belief that there was a justice; and in this I was not wrong; for there is one insofar as God has been willing to reveal it to us. But this is not the way I thought of it and this is where I was wrong; for I believed that our justice was basically just and that I was capable of knowing and judging it."

N. (The Hellenes.) "Daring of noble races, mad, absurd, spontaneous daring . . . their indifference and their scorn for every security of the body, for life and comfort."

Novel. "Love is fulfilled or it degrades. The more it is thwarted, the greater is the mutilation it eventually leaves. If love is not creative, it prevents any true creation forever. It is a tyrant and a petty tyrant. Consequently P. suffered from having become involved in loving without being able to give all to that love. In that mad waste of time and of soul, he recognized a sort of justice which in the end was the only one he had ever really encountered on this earth. But to recognize that justice was also to recognize a duty: the duty of raising that love, and themselves, above the petty, of accepting the most terrible but the frankest anguish, the kind that had always made him withdraw with pounding heart, filled with cowardice. He could do no more nor be otherwise, and the only love that would have saved all was a love that would have accepted him for what he was. But love cannot accept what is. That's not the reason it cries out everywhere on earth. It cries out to refuse kindness, compassion, intelligence, everything that leads to compromise. It cries out toward the impossible, the absolute, the sky on fire, inexhaustible springtime, life after death, and death itself transfigured in eternal life. How could *he* have been accepted in love, he who was only misery in a certain way, and awareness of that misery? He alone could accept himself—by accepting the long, interminable, and painful suffering of losing love and knowing that he had lost it through his own fault. That was his freedom, bathed in a terrible blood, to be sure. But it was also the condition for something at least to be created within the limits that belonged to him, in the consecration of his own misery and of the misery of any life, but also in the effort toward nobility that alone justified it.

"Short of that torture, any weakness makes love look childish and stupid, makes of it that empty, pale restraint at which even a slightly exacting heart eventually baulks. Yes, this is what should be said: 'I love you—but I am nothing, or very little, and you cannot really accept me despite all your love, for basically, deep within you, you demand all and I neither have nor am all; forgive me for having less soul than love, less luck than desire, and for loving beyond my reach. Forgive me and cease humiliating me. When you are no longer capable of love for me, you will be capable of justice. Then you will measure my hell and you will love me above ourselves with a love that will never be able to suffice me either but which I shall nonetheless attribute to life, to accept it once more, in anguish.' Yes, this was right, but then the hardest began. With her absent, the days cried out, every night was a wound."

The strongest passion of the twentieth century: slavery.

At Brou, the reclining statues of Marguerite of Austria and Philibert of Savoie, instead of facing the sky, are facing each other eternally.[9]

Whoever has not insisted upon absolute virginity in people and the world, and screamed with nostalgia and impotence at the impossibility of achieving it, whoever has not been destroyed through trying to love, as second best, a face that cannot invent love and merely repeats it, cannot understand the reality of revolt and its rage to destroy.[1]

Action Française. Mentality of history's outcasts: resentment. Race theory of the political ghetto.

I don't like others' secrets. But I am interested in their confessions.

[9] The ornate late-Gothic church of Brou at Bourg-en-Bresse with its elaborate tomb is a memorial to Marguerite's love for her husband.
[1] See *The Rebel* (Alfred A. Knopf, 1954), p. 230.

Play: A man without personality. And he changes according to the image others offer him of himself. Poor dishrag with his wife. Intelligent and courageous with the woman he loves, etc. . . . Finally one day the two images conflict. In the end:

The maid: "Monsieur is very good."

He: "Here, Marie, this is for you."

Few people capable of *understanding* art.

In the time of Rembrandt, the commercial artists paint battle scenes.

Paris. The wind and rain have hurled the autumn leaves onto the pavement. You walk on a damp, tawny fur.

A Negro taxi driver, exceptionally courteous for the Paris of 1950, says to me as we pass in front of the Comédie-Française surrounded by cars: "The House of Molière is full tonight."

For the past two thousand years the Greek value has been constantly and persistently slandered. In this regard Marxism took over from Christianity. And for two thousand years the Greek value has resisted to such a degree that, under its ideologies, the twentieth century is more Greek and pagan than Christian and Russian.

Intellectuals make the theory and the masses make the economy. In the end the intellectuals make use of the masses and through them the theory makes use of the economy. This is why they must maintain the state of siege and the economic enslavement—so that the masses will remain manual laborers. It is quite true that economics make up the matter of history. Ideas are satisfied with directing it.

Henceforth I knew the truth about myself and about others. But I could not accept it. I writhed under it, burned red-hot.

The creators. They will have to fight at first, when the catastrophe comes. If the result is defeat, the survivors will go to lands where it will be possible to assemble culture again: Chile, Mexico, etc. If it's victory: the greatest danger.

Eighteenth century: To conclude that man is perfectible is itself debatable. But to conclude, after having lived, that man is good . . .

Yes, I have a native land: the French language.

Novel
1) Capture of Weimar, or the equivalent, by those who have been struck off the list.[2]
2) In the camp a proud intellectual is subjected to the

2 Probably those deported to concentration camps.

spitting cell.[3] His whole life from that moment on: to survive in order to be able to kill.

Dissolution of the group.[4] Lazarevitch: "We love one another, that's true. Incapable of raising a finger for what we love. No, we are not powerless. But we refuse to do even the little we could do. A meeting is a nuisance, if it's raining, if we have had trouble at home, etc., etc. . . . ."

Dishonesty of the artist when he pretends to believe in the democracy of principles. For then he negates the most basic thing in his experience, which is the great lesson of art: hierarchy and order. The fact that such dishonesty is sentimental doesn't help. It leads to the slavery of factories and concentration camps.

S. Weil is right; it's not the human being that must be protected, but the possibilities within him. Moreover, she says, "one doesn't enter truth without having passed through one's own annihilation, without having lived at length in a state of total and extreme humiliation." The misfortune (a chance can wipe me out) is that state of humiliation, not anguish. And again: "The spirit of justice and the spirit of truth are one."

The revolutionary spirit rejects original sin. By so doing, it sinks into it. The Greek spirit doesn't think of it. By so doing, it escapes it.

3 See *The Fall* (Alfred A. Knopf, 1957), pp. 10–11, where the spitting cell is described.
4 The group of Liaisons Internationales founded to succor the victims of any totalitarian regime.

Madmen in concentration camps. At liberty, the butt of cruel jokes.

During the flogging, at Buchenwald, an opera singer is forced to sing his great arias.

Id. Jehovah's witnesses, at Buchenwald, refused to take part in the collection of woolens for the German army.

At Hinzert, the French prisoners wore two capital letters on their clothing: H N for Hunde-Nation: nation of dogs.

It's because France is a military nation that Communism has a chance there.

Play.
"That's honesty for you. It does harm while thinking it's doing good."
"Yes, but it's distinguishing."

The principle of law is that of the State. Roman principle that 1789 reintroduced into the world through force and against the right. We must return to the Greek principle, which is autonomy.

Text on the sea. The waves, saliva of the gods. The sea monster, the sea to be overcome, etc. My excessive liking for pleasure.

Alexandre Jacob: "A mother, you see, is humanity."

Leibniz: "I despise almost nothing."

JANUARY 23, '51 — Valence

I had shouted, demanded, exulted, despaired. But at the age of thirty-seven, one day I made the acquaintance of misfortune and found out what, despite appearances, I had not known until then. Around the middle of my life I had to learn all over again painfully how to live alone.

Novel. "I who had lived so long, bewailing, in the world of the flesh, admired those like S.W. who seemed to escape it. As far as I was concerned, I could not imagine a love without possession, hence without the humiliating anguish that belongs to those who live according to the flesh. I went so far as to prefer that a person who loved me should preserve physical fidelity rather than that of the soul and the heart. I was well enough aware that for a woman the latter fidelity conditions the former and I used to insist on it then, but merely as the condition of that exclusive possession that mattered more to me than all the rest. It was my personal salvation, for being deprived of it was an endless source of torture. My paradise lay in the virginity of others."

Grasse, the capital of hairdressers' assistants.

Go back to the passage from Hellenism to Christianity, the true and only turning point in history. Essay on fate (Nemesis?).

Collection philosophical essays. Philosophy of expression+commentary first book of Ethics+reflections on Hegel (lectures on philosophy of history)+Grenier essay+ commentary Apology of Socrates.

"Liberty is a gift of the sea." Proudhon.

What I have so long sought becomes apparent at last. Dying becomes a consent.

February 5. To die without having settled anything. But who dies having settled everything, except . . . ? To settle at least the peace of those one has loved . . . To oneself nothing is due, not even (especially not) death in peace.

February 1951.[5] *The Rebel.* I wanted to tell the truth without ceasing to be generous. That's my justification.

Work, etc. 1) Essay on the sea. Put together book of essays: The Holiday. 2) Preface to American edition of Plays. 3) Preface to American edition of essays.[6] 4) Translation *Timon of Athens.* 5) Love of the remote. 6) The eternal voice.

[5] The manuscript reads 1950, but this is presumably an error.
[6] Camus did indeed write brief but significant prefaces for the Alfred A. Knopf editions of *The Myth of Sisyphus and Other Essays* (1955) and *Caligula and Three Other Plays* (1958). Apparently he never translated the Shakespeare play.

Ignatius Loyola: "Conversation is a sin if it is disordered."

After *The Rebel.* Aggressive, obstinate rejection of the system. The aphorism henceforth.

Loyola. The human race: "Those men in a body moving toward hell."

Short story. The anguish of death. And he commits suicide.

Petty breed of Parisian writers who cultivate what they believe to be insolence. Servants who at one and the same time ape the great and mock them in the pantry.

I used to long at times for a violent death—as a death which excuses one from crying out at the tearing away of the soul. At other times I would dream of a protracted and constantly lucid end so that it could not be said at least that I had been taken by surprise—in my absence—to find out, in short . . . But one stifles, in the earth.

MARCH 1, '51
It's by delaying his conclusions, even when they seem to him evident, that a philosopher progresses.

A spectacular virtue that leads to denying one's passions. A higher virtue that leads to balancing them.

My powerful native tendency for forgetting.

If I were to die unknown to the world, in the depths of a cold prison, at the last moment the sea would fill my cell, would come and raise me above myself and help me to die without hate.[7]

MARCH 7, 1951

Finished the first writing of *The Rebel*. With this book the first two cycles come to an end. Thirty-seven years old. And now, can creation be free?

Any fulfillment is a bondage. It obliges one to a higher fulfillment.

[7] See "La Mer au plus près" in *L'Été*.

BIOGRAPHICAL NOTE

The dates spanned by Volume Two of the *Notebooks* include the second half of the war and the adjustment of the succeeding years. At the beginning of this period, Albert Camus was a young journalist living on a mountain farm in central France. His tubercular condition, diagnosed as early as 1930, had kept him from active service in the war. Yet he had gone from his native Algeria to Paris in March 1940 as managing editor of the daily *Paris-Soir*, after the closing of the Algerian paper where he had begun his journalistic career. Then had come the exodus from Paris, during which he and his paper had moved to Clermont-Ferrand in the so-called "Free Zone." In January 1941 he had returned to Algeria, then a part of Metropolitan France, with his young wife, whom he had married in Lyons a month earlier, to teach in a private school in Oran. There he had finished his essay *The Myth of Sisyphus*, as he had earlier finished his novel *The Stranger*, during the exodus.

When he returned to the mainland of France in the summer of 1941, without his wife and without a specific plan, he was moved chiefly by considerations of health. To return to that war-torn, enemy-patrolled country when all who could were leaving it required courage. Plans for the publication of his two books in Paris in 1942 were already simmering, but his was not simply the classic case of the sensitive youth blossoming in his remote province and then being drawn inevitably to the capital. Nor was he yet a member of the Resistance with a precise role to play; he tells us himself that only the execution of the former Deputy Gabriel Péri in December 1941 caused him to see the need for a civilian Resistance.

Soon after settling in the spring of 1942 in the mountains near Le Chambon-sur-Lignon, from where he could reach the city of Saint-Étienne for regular treatments, he began meeting other scattered writers such as Francis Ponge and the young poet René Leynaud, who was later caught and executed as an underground leader. The Allied landing in North Africa on the eleventh of November 1942 prevented him from returning home. He did not see his wife or his mother for the duration of the hostilities.

In November 1943 Camus, now the author of two much discussed books published in 1942 in Paris (*L'Etranger* and *Le Mythe de Sisyphe*), moved to Paris, where a position as editor in the Gallimard publishing house provided a *raison d'être*. He joined Pascal Pia, with whom he had already worked on *Alger-Républicain* and *Paris-Soir*, in editing the clandestine paper *Combat*. Then it was that he began to occupy André Gide's apartment at 1 bis rue Vaneau, vacated by its owner, who had gone to safer regions.

From late 1943 until the Germans were driven out of France, Albert Camus played an ever more important and increasingly dangerous role as a highly articulate spokesman for the intellectual underground and as a member of an intelligence network. Even though many of his friends and associates were arrested, often tortured and executed, he carried on with his stirring editorials and his day-to-day clandestine activities. The public read his anonymous writings with the same avidity and the same sense of danger with which they listened to the *verboten* news broadcast by the BBC. Foreseeing the Liberation, Camus planned long in advance and then at the strategic moment took over by force the printing plant of a big collaborationist newspaper so that his own *Combat* could appear openly in a suitable format while the last enemy pockets were being wiped out.

Throughout 1942 and 1943, while reading widely in all literatures, Camus was already writing his novel *La Peste* (*The Plague*) and his second play, *Le Malentendu* (*The Misunderstanding*), under the unlikely title of *Budejovice*. The same passion for the theater which had made him start his own acting company at the age of twenty-three and direct plays in Algerian cities led him to rewrite his first play, *Caligula*, the first draft of which was done largely in 1938. Yet clandestine journalism still occupied much of his time. The first of his stirring *Lettres à un ami allemand* (included in *Resistance, Rebellion, and Death*) appeared in the underground *Revue Libre* in 1943. In November of that year, Camus reached the age of thirty.

August 1944 marked the Liberation of Paris and the end of the shameful Occupation. But before then Camus had met Sartre and had seen the joint publication of his own two plays in May and the presentation of the new one, *Le Malentendu*, at the Mathurins Theater with Maria Casarès and Marcel Herrand in the chief roles. He was deeply moved by the execution of his friend René Leynaud in June and had assumed the editorship of *Combat* even before it could be published openly in August. Meanwhile he continued writing *La Peste* and began *L'Homme révolté* (*The Rebel*).

In 1945 the first fragment of *L'Homme révolté* was published in a collection of contemporary metaphysical writings entitled *L'Existence*. In October *Caligula* was finally staged at the Hébertot Theater with the young Gérard Philipe in the title role. That fall Camus revisited the village of Lourmarin, near Aix-en-Provence, where in 1958, after he won the Nobel Prize, he bought a house, and where he is now buried.

From March to May 1946, Albert Camus traveled in North America; he had given up the editorship of *Combat*, although he continued to write for it sporadically. The periodical *L'Arche* published "The Minotaur or the Stop in Oran," which was included in his book *L'Été* (*Summer*). Late in the year he held dialogues in Paris with Malraux, Sartre, and others about the role of the intellectual in politics.

In early 1947 he again assumed the editorship of *Combat*, but he soon handed it over to Claude Bourdet. In June, Gallimard published *La Peste*, which won the Prix des Critiques. That summer the posthumous poems of René Leynaud also appeared, with a preface by Camus. Again, for reasons of health, he returned to Panelier near Le Chambon-sur-Lignon.

Except for a trip to Algeria in February, 1948 was devoted to writing the play *Les Justes* (*The Just Assassins*) and working on the long essay *L'Homme révolté*. Late in the year, at the Marigny Theater, Jean-Louis Barrault presented *L'État de siège* (*State of Siege*), the play on which he had been such a help to Camus.

In December 1949 *Les Justes* was presented at the Hébertot Theater, with Serge Reggiani and Maria Casarès.

Les Justes and *Actuelles I*, a collection of Camus's earlier political articles (see *Resistance, Rebellion, and Death*), were both published in 1950. During that year Camus spent much time in convalescence at Cabris near the South Coast of France and in the Vosges Mountains. In Paris he settled into an apartment on the rue Madame.

When this volume of *Notebooks* ends, Camus had just finished *L'Homme révolté*. Its publication later that year of 1951 stirred up a storm of controversy. In November 1951 Camus became thirty-eight.

Justin O'Brien